# A Cowboy's Justice

## Lisa Childs

## LOVE INSPIRED
### INSPIRATIONAL ROMANCE

# LOVE INSPIRED®

## INSPIRATIONAL ROMANCE

Recycling programs
for this product may
not exist in your area.

ISBN-13: 978-1-335-55599-1

A Cowboy's Justice

Copyright © 2023 by Lisa Childs

For questions and comments about the quality of this book, please contact us
at CustomerService@Harlequin.com.

Love Inspired
22 Adelaide St. West, 41st Floor
Toronto, Ontario M5H 4E3, Canada
www.LoveInspired.com

Printed in U.S.A.

A good man sheweth favour, and lendeth:
he will guide his affairs with discretion.
—*Psalm* 112:5

With great appreciation for all my siblings,
Helen, Phyllis, Chris, Mike, Jackie and Tony,
and the unbreakable bond we share! Love you all!

## Chapter One

The sound of the hooves pounding against the ground echoed the pounding of Ryder Lewis's heart inside his chest. He gripped the reins tighter in his gloved hands as he urged his mount faster across the snow-capped hills and through the valleys of the expansive campus toward the entrance of the private college.

*She* was coming back.

Maybe now he would finally get the justice he'd sought, with no success, for the past decade. Justice had eluded him because of her. Because she was the key...

Maybe now he would finally convince her to tell the truth, to admit to what really happened that night so long ago. But he had to be patient, like he'd been all these years. He couldn't push it; he couldn't push *her*. So he eased back on the reins and slowed the horse. He needed to draw up, turn around and ride Sable back to the stable. He couldn't meet her car and confront her like he wanted.

He had to wait until their paths crossed naturally.

And he would make sure they crossed. He'd worked too hard to track her down, and then to get her back here, to lose her again. With as long as he'd already waited for justice, it was excruciating to continue to bide his time until he had the chance to get the truth out of her and get her to admit it to the authorities.

That she'd lied.

That she had aided and abetted a killer…and for all these years that killer had gone free. And no justice had been served for the murder committed ten years ago on this campus, for the brutal murder of his younger sister…

Kristy Kendall found her foot lifting up from the accelerator the closer she got to the gates of the private college in northern Michigan. She had vowed never to come back here. At least not while awake.

When she slept, she often returned here in her dreams…in her nightmares…

Nightmare.

She only had one.

The same one over and over again.

That moment she'd opened the door to the small apartment she'd shared with Mara Lewis on the campus of St. Michel's Private College and had found her…dead.

Brutally murdered.

The scream she'd uttered then, the same scream she uttered when she had the nightmare, burned the back of her throat. But she forced it down with a deep breath. A chill chased down her spine with the memory and she shivered.

If only she had been there that night.

If only...

But she couldn't change the past. She could focus only on the present. And this job was a present she hadn't been able to refuse. If she didn't accept it, she was at risk of having to file for bankruptcy over her student loans and the possible repossession of her vehicle, such as it was. The motor of the Chevrolet rumbled and clunked as she pulled through the open gate in the middle of the fieldstone archway entrance of St. Michel's Private College.

The school, in the upper peninsula of Michigan, encompassed more than a hundred acres of woods and hills, with several brick and fieldstone buildings spread across the campus, brick-paved trails winding between them. Kristy shivered again as she remembered walking along those paths in winter, snow falling so hard she could barely see where the trail was, the drifts so deep that snow made it over the tops of her boots and down inside, dampening her socks and feet.

This early in the spring just small patches of snow clung to the brown grass here and there and to the tops of the tallest pine trees. In the distance, between those pines, she spied something moving. An animal...

Not a deer or a bear, which she'd spotted on the campus in the past. This was a pale brown horse, and on its back was a rider, wearing a tan suede jacket and a black cowboy hat. And the sight of him stunned her.

It couldn't be.

*He* wouldn't still be here, not ten years after the murder. Surely he would have returned to his life, to the rodeo...

He wouldn't be here yet, looking for Mara's killer. She was probably just imagining it was him because Ryder Lewis was the first cowboy she'd ever met in person. As a child of missionaries, she'd spent more time in third world countries than she had in the US until she'd been fortunate enough to get accepted to St. Michel's. Sometimes this campus had seemed as remote and untouched as the villages where she'd grown up until that day.

Maybe thinking that she'd seen Ryder here was an indication that she had to face the past, that she couldn't keep running from it like she'd tried. And maybe that was another reason she'd accepted this adjunct professor position, not just for the steady paycheck for teaching the creative writing course, but also for the truth. She'd spent the past ten years wondering what it was.

While she'd never forgotten that night, there was so much of it she didn't remember. If only she'd come back to their apartment after that party....

If only she'd never gone to that party at all....

Maybe she could have saved Mara.

Instead, she'd betrayed her.

Her best friend. The best friend she'd ever had. And she would never forgive herself for that, and she knew that *he* wouldn't forgive her either. Ryder Lewis had made it clear at his sister's memorial service that he also held her responsible for his sister's killer going free. She blamed herself because she wasn't there to stop the killer or at least provide a description of him. Ryder blamed her because he thought he knew who the killer was. But he was wrong.

Was the real killer still here? Somewhere in the town of Eagle Valley, Michigan? Or had he just been passing through the area, as campus security and the state police had believed? Had he gone on to other towns, committing other senseless murders?

Mara's brother should have been looking for him. The real killer.

But instead, he'd been looking for her.

She knew it because family and friends had warned her over the years about a man calling them, trying to find out where she was currently living. That man had had a deep voice with a slight southern twang.

Ryder Lewis.

No other man would have been calling around for her. She didn't have any ex-boyfriends that would have been trying to track her down. Besides meeting up for a cup of coffee or to study, she'd never really dated. Before Mara's murder, she'd been too shy and introverted to put herself out there that way. And after…

She hadn't felt like she deserved to be happy when Mara couldn't be.

So Ryder was the only one who could have been trying to find her. But for what purpose? She couldn't tell him what she didn't know, and she wouldn't lie for him to make a case against an innocent man.

The windshield was grimy and stained with bugs and road salt, so she had to peer hard through her glasses to see the horse and rider as they grew smaller and smaller with distance. Was that him now?

Astride that horse?

Riding around the campus...like Mara had said he used to ride around his family ranch and then the rodeo arena. Why would he be here, unless he had somehow known she was coming?

That chill chased down her spine again, but instead of shivering, perspiration trailed down her back. She wasn't hot because of the car's heat; barely any wafted from the wide-open vents of her beat-up clunker. For some reason, just the thought of Ryder Lewis made her sweat. The first time Mara had showed her a picture of her older brother, warmth had flooded Kristy's face, along with incredulity that the man wasn't a movie star. He was so good-looking, with shiny black hair and piercing blue eyes, that he could have been famous. Well, more famous.

After his stint in the Marines had ended, he'd found success as a rodeo rider; that was why he hadn't been able to get away to visit his younger sister. And once he'd found the time, it had been too late.

Kristy had met him at the memorial for Mara in the little fieldstone church on campus. After that service, he'd given her such a hard time. He'd been so angry.

Kristy couldn't blame him for how upset he'd been with her; she was upset with herself but for different reasons. She wasn't lying like he believed, like she wished she was. She really was the alibi for the person Ryder was unjustifiably convinced had killed his sister: Mara's boyfriend, Skip Holdren. Was Skip still living on the family estate that adjoined the college campus?

Was anyone else around from back then besides the man who'd offered Kristy the position? Why would *he* have offered it to her?

She hesitated for a moment, her foot entirely off the accelerator. Should she turn around and leave?

Could anything good really come of being back here?

The truth.

It was past time that Kristy figured out what that was. And not just about ten years ago, but also about herself and about this job. She eased her foot back down on the gas pedal and steered the car down the winding drive and into an empty parking spot outside the old brick administration building.

Here, in the distance, she could see something other than a horse and rider. Between pine trees, above one of the rolling hills, was the steeple of the little fieldstone church where she'd prayed so often. Before Mara's murder, she'd prayed for her future, so that all her dreams would come true. After Mara's murder, she'd prayed her nightmare wasn't real, that it hadn't really happened, and she would return to the little apartment she'd shared with Mara and find her dancing around their living room, singing off-key and smiling as brightly as she always had.

Until that day.

She hadn't been smiling then.

Kristy closed her eyes, trying to shut out that image…

that nightmare. But it persisted, haunting her mind while she was awake like it so often haunted her nights. Mara lying in the middle of all that blood...her beautiful green eyes open and staring up at her in shock and horror.

The scream tickled the back of Kristy's throat, begging to be released, but she sucked in a breath, trying to hold it down along with the cup of truck stop coffee she'd had a while ago. A rap against the glass of the driver's side window startled her so much that she released the scream. Then she jumped, and the seat belt she had yet to release snapped against her neck, biting into her skin. She whirled toward the window, half expecting to see Mara standing there, with those glazed eyes fixed in that empty stare.

Or Ryder.

But if that had been him on the horse, he'd been riding away from the administration building, across campus in the other direction, probably toward the stables where the equestrian team had boarded their horses. A man stood outside her car, peering inside her window. With dark eyes that crinkled at the corners as he smiled at her, he looked nothing like Ryder Lewis.

She released a shaky breath and rolled down her window.

"I'm sorry I startled you," he said. "I was just returning from lunch and saw you sitting here and realized you're probably waiting for me."

She recognized the voice more than the face. Now she smiled, too. "Professor Stolz..." Except he wasn't a professor anymore. He was the dean. Her face flushed with embarrassment over her faux pas. "Uh, I mean, Dean…" Dean was actually his first name, though, if she remembered correctly.

Kristy had only taken one of his classes. Mara had been the one who'd signed up for everything he'd taught, as had every other female student at St. Michel's. She'd been lucky to get into that one class. Business or marketing… She couldn't remember now what he'd taught. But teaching hadn't been his end goal, which he'd made clear in that class. Running the place had been.

Then she realized that he must have moved up from dean, on to provost, or he wouldn't have had the authority to extend the job offer to her since creative writing wouldn't have fallen within his department. Given the small size of the private college, the provost pretty much ran the place while the president worked at procuring more funding. So Dean Stolz had achieved his dreams.

What was his reason for reaching out to her? Sending that letter to her with the offer of teaching the next semester?

While she'd achieved one of her dreams, she had only the one book published, and it hadn't done nearly as well as she'd hoped it would. So it wasn't as if she had the publishing credits of other creative writing teachers. While adjunct professors were only required to have a master's degree, which she had, they were hired more for having expertise in the field or on the subject they were being hired to teach.

"Please, call me Dean, and I'll call you Kristy," the

provost said with a charming grin that had dimples piercing his lean cheeks. Then he straightened up and reached for her door.

More embarrassment flooded her as the handle nearly came off in his grasp. Maybe it wouldn't be a great loss if the vehicle was repossessed. She quickly opened it herself and nearly struck him with the door before he stepped back. Then she slid out from beneath the steering wheel, wishing she'd had time to at least check her reflection in the rearview mirror before meeting her new boss. Some of her long hair had slipped free of the too-loose bun because brown tendrils fell across her cheek and over one of the lenses of her glasses. She pushed the tortoiseshell frames back up her nose and held out her hand.

He took it in his and held it instead of shaking it. "I hope you weren't waiting for me long."

She shook her head, which tugged more hair loose from the bun. She pulled her hand free of his to brush back the strands. "I just arrived," she assured him. "I haven't even gone inside yet."

Despite knowing that she needed to deal with the past, she still wasn't sure she was ready or that she wanted to be here. But along with a steady paycheck for this term, she would also have a place to live in one of the small apartments on campus. It would be in the faculty building, not where she'd stayed with Mara. And she would have a lot of time to write and reflect and maybe to remember.

Not that she believed there was anything else to recall. She hadn't been at their place when Mara had died. Instead of helping and protecting her best friend, she'd been busy betraying her. And she would never forgive herself for failing Mara.

"Is it strange?" he asked, and he stared intently at her as if studying her face. And as he did, his grin slipped away, making her wonder if the smile had been sincere or practiced. "Being back here?"

She shivered and nodded. But strange was the least of it.

It was scary. And heartbreaking and maybe long overdue.

# *Chapter Two*

Had she seen him? Ryder should have been more careful, more patient, but he'd already been looking for her for too long so that he could get her to finally tell the truth.

He dropped into the chair across from his friend's desk and wondered if Kristy had used it during the meeting with her new boss. There was another chair next to it, also in brown leather like the one behind Dean's desk, but with a lower back. The walls of the office were brown, too, paneled and highly polished like the desk and the floor. A patterned low-pile rug broke up some of the monotony of the space, as did the two big windows in the corner of the office.

Outside, the light was already beginning to fade as the days were short yet. Dean never left early, though, and neither did Ryder.

"How'd it go?" he asked his friend. He and the provost went way back to boot camp where they'd bonded for life.

Dean had just been a reserve, though, while Ryder had signed up for a six-year enlistment. Dean's plan had always been to become a professor and someday a provost. When he'd achieved that professional goal a few years ago, he'd called Ryder—who at thirty-five had been ready to retire from the rodeo—and offered the former Marine MP the head of campus security position. But Dean had offered Ryder even more than a job; he'd given him the opportunity to finally get the justice for Mara that he'd been denied so long. That *she* had been denied so long.

Dean leaned back his leather chair and sighed. "She's clearly suspicious of my reasons for sending her the offer of employment."

"Then she's not stupid," Ryder remarked, which comforted him somewhat since he'd had such a problem finding her all these years. "Did she ask?"

Dean shook his head. "No."

Then maybe she hadn't seen him, or if she had, she hadn't realized it was him. They'd only seen each other in person that one time…at the memorial. And he doubted she'd tried to find him. It would have been easy enough when he'd been on the circuit to look online to see the rodeo he'd been signed up to ride in. Then for the last three years, he'd been here.

While his main reason for accepting this position had been to prove the guilt of his sister's killer, he'd also taken his job seriously to ensure the safety of all the students on campus. He hadn't wanted anyone else to lose someone they loved like he and his family had lost Mara. Completely overhauling the security department had kept him very busy. At least that was the excuse he gave himself for not getting justice yet for Mara.

But now that it was closing in on the ten-year anniversary of her death, he couldn't wait any longer. *She* couldn't wait any longer.

Ryder had really believed his younger sister would be safe here, at this small private college where his friend had been teaching classes. He'd been wrong then, but he wasn't wrong now. Not about Kristy Kendall. She was the key to justice.

"She was strictly professional, kept the conversation about the class curriculum," Dean continued.

Ryder peered across the desk at his recently divorced friend. "Did you try to make the conversation personal?" Dean had a reputation for being a flirt, but that was just his personality; he charmed everyone.

That wasn't a problem Ryder had ever had; his reputation was for being brusque and sometimes brutally honest.

"I tried to gauge how she feels about being back here," Dean said. "But she didn't answer my question about that."

Ryder could imagine and remembered how hard it had been for him to drive through that stone archway onto St. Michel's campus, his horse in a trailer behind the truck. He'd felt like he had that day... that horrible day he'd come to bring his sister's body home, to take part in the memorial for her in that little campus church.

To him, it was like Mara had just been murdered or had been murdered all over again.

"You would know," Dean remarked. He knew Ryder well, too well sometimes. "When are you going to talk to her?"

Ryder sighed. "If she's already suspicious, I need to bide my time. I don't want her to quit and run away again."

"She didn't run away," Dean said. "She stayed for another year. She graduated with her bachelor's degree in literary arts."

Ryder flinched as guilt jabbed his heart. He was the one who'd run away, who'd returned to the rodeo after bringing his sister's ashes home to the ranch in Texas where they'd grown up. He'd been so convinced that justice would happen, that the state police and the former head of campus security would keep their promise to bring Mara's killer to justice. But they'd failed her, just like he'd failed her.

"So you think she'll stick around?" Ryder asked.

Dean shrugged again. "I don't know. You have."

"I'm not leaving until there is justice for Mara," he said. Maybe if he hadn't left after the memorial that day, she would have had it already. Maybe he would have already found the evidence to prove her former boyfriend's guilt and Kristy Kendall's complicity in providing him a false alibi.

Dean leaned back so far in his chair that it creaked in protest. "So I'm going to have to find another head of security soon?"

"I hope so," Ryder said. That was his fervent wish...

that he could finally find justice for Mara and, hopefully, with it would come peace for her and him. But the journey toward that felt like a rodeo.

He'd been waiting around for a long time and now he was finally climbing into the chute, about to climb onto the back of the bull, and soon that gate would open.

And it was going to be eight seconds of fear and adrenaline and chaos.

If he was lucky.

The lights in the parking lot flickered on as the last of the day slipped into night. Then the bulbs all flickered off again, threatening to leave her in the dark. Like she was about her new position at St. Michel's.

She should have asked Dean Stolz why he'd really extended that job offer. But Kristy was afraid he would have told her the truth, that despite her master's degree in English, she didn't have enough real-world experience as a writer to be qualified to teach creative writing even as an adjunct professor. Sure, she'd written a book—most of it right here on this campus—but that had been before the murder. She hadn't written much since then, just some articles for magazines.

Mostly she'd waited tables to earn enough money to visit her parents in whatever country they were working. Maybe she should have just stayed with them the last time; she'd wanted to because she'd actually felt useful then, her life purposeful like theirs were. But they'd urged her to go back to the States, back to the life they knew she'd always wanted.

But all that had changed when Mara had lost her life. Then, instead of bringing Kristy happiness, any success she'd had, like the book and those articles, had brought on guilt instead. Even this teaching job churned guilt in Kristy's empty stomach. Because she knew she hadn't earned it.

But if she'd asked the provost and he'd told her the truth, she wouldn't have known what to do. It wasn't as if she could have proudly turned down the job, especially the apartment. She had nowhere else to go.

The lights buzzed and flickered back on, and she released the breath she hadn't realized she'd been holding. Then she jammed the key into the trunk's lock and pushed up the lid. She'd already brought in most of her things—some battered boxes she'd dragged around with her for the past ten years. With as much as she moved, she should have had a set of luggage or at least a trunk. But the boxes were lighter and easier to carry. She grabbed the last one and slammed the lid closed. Then she headed back toward the faculty housing in the big red brick building. It looked much the same as the dorms, the other campus apartments and even the classroom buildings.

And instead of feeling like a teacher, she felt like a student again at thirty. Most other people her age probably had a home and a family.

Mara would have. She'd been that beautiful, that driven...that exceptional. Everyone had been so drawn to Mara, falling instantly in love with her.

Tears stung Kristy's eyes, but she blinked them back. Mara had hated to see anyone sad, but more than that she'd hated to see anyone bored. A smile curved Kristy's lips as she allowed herself to remember her old friend before that day…before that tragedy.

She'd been so fun-loving and so much fun herself. Just studying with Mara or making dinner together had made Kristy laugh more than she ever had before. She hadn't laughed like that—that uproariously, that joyously—since Mara's death.

Kristy's smile slipped away, and she released an unsteady sigh. She'd known that coming back here was going to have her thinking about Mara even more than she usually did, and she'd thought she could handle that—thought that she might finally be able to deal with the past. But it wasn't just Mara she was thinking about with her return. For some reason, Ryder Lewis was on her mind, to the point that she must have conjured up the sight of that horse and rider from her imagination.

It wasn't that far-fetched, though, since there was a horse stable on campus for the equestrian team. Mara had been on that team and had worked at the stables as part of her scholarship. But the rider Kristy thought she'd seen had been wearing a cowboy hat, not the riding hats the equestrian team wore.

Could it have been him?

She shook her head in denial. What would Ryder be doing here after all this time?

In just a few weeks, it would be the ten-year anniversary of Mara's murder. It didn't seem possible she'd been gone that long. But even back then, when Kristy had found her body, she hadn't believed it was possible that anyone could have wanted to kill Mara Lewis.

The tears stung her eyes again, but she blinked them away and focused on the present. On settling into her new apartment. Using her back, she pushed open the door to the building foyer. She'd left a small block in the jamb to hold it open, so she wouldn't have to unlock it again. She'd done the same to her apartment. But when she climbed the stairs and walked down the hall toward that door, she found it shut tight.

Had the block slipped out? Had someone closed it for her?

Fortunately she'd already put the apartment key on the ring with her other ones, so she propped the box on her hip and dug the keys out of pocket. She unlocked and pushed open the door and let out a small scream of shock.

The chaos she saw reminded her of that day she'd let herself into the apartment she'd shared with Mara. Of the pictures knocked off the wall, of the cutlery and glasses strewn across the kitchen floor. Of the way she'd found her friend. That scene had been so much worse than what she saw now.

The boxes she'd dropped just inside the door during her previous trips were upended, the contents spilled across the hardwood floor. The cardboard was crushed, as if someone had stomped the boxes after emptying them. Maybe it was that show of anger, of violence, that reminded her of how she'd found Mara.

Whoever had done this had been filled with rage. Why? And who?

She'd only been gone a short while to retrieve the last box from her car. How had someone done all this?

Her heart pounded hard and fast as fear filled her. Scared that the person was still inside the apartment, she backed toward the door to the hall. And as she did, she caught sight of her reflection in the mirror hanging on the wall. Her face was pale, her eyes wide behind her glasses, but her image was marred by the words scrawled across the glass.

*You shouldn't have come back!*

Kristy couldn't help but agree. She shouldn't have come back. This was a mistake. And she hadn't needed the note, or her belongings tossed about, to prove that to her. But someone had gone to all that trouble.

Was that person still inside the place?

*Please, God, keep me safe...*

She dropped the box she held and turned toward the door, desperate to escape before she wound up like Mara had that night so long ago...

Dead.

## Chapter Three

Ryder had thought he'd have to find some excuse to run into her, an innocent way of crossing paths with her, so that he didn't frighten her off. He certainly hadn't expected her to call him. Well, she actually called campus security, but he had a program on his phone that sent him a transcript of every call as it came into dispatch.

*"This is Kristy Kendall. Someone got into my apartment and vandalized my things and...left a disturbing note...and I'm not sure if they're gone..."*

Ryder had hung around the administration building for a while even after Dean had left him for another meeting, so he was close to the faculty apartments—so close that he arrived there within minutes on foot. He'd left Sable in her stall earlier, and his truck was parked in the lot near the campus security offices. It would have taken him longer to retrieve it than to run to Kristy's apartment building to make sure she wasn't in danger. The fear of someone hurting her had his blood pumping even harder and faster than it was from running to her. He worked so hard to keep the campus safe because he didn't want anyone getting hurt, but for some reason, he especially didn't want Kristy getting hurt.

She was in the parking lot, where the dispatcher had told her to wait for campus security, standing next to that clunker he'd suspected was hers when it had driven through the fieldstone arch earlier today. Even from the back, he recognized her long rich brown hair, bound up in a messy bun on the back of her head. Mara had snapchatted him so many pictures of Kristy studying with her hair just like that. Her small body trembled, either shaking with fear or cold. Then she turned and saw him, and her brown eyes widened behind the lenses of her glasses.

"It was you..." she murmured.

He didn't know if she was referring to seeing him earlier on his horse or if she thought he was the one who'd vandalized her place. While he was angry with her for lying for Skip Holdren, he didn't want to hurt her or frighten her. "Are you okay?" he asked. "I just got the call about the break-in at your place."

Her brow furrowed beneath the strands of dark hair that had slipped out of her bun. "How? I called campus security."

"I am campus security," he said.

The color drained from her face, leaving her ghostly pale in the glow of the parking lot lights. Clearly she wasn't reassured.

"I got the report that there was someone in your

apartment," he said. "And you're not sure if they're still there. Did you see anyone inside?"

She shook her head. "But I didn't go more than a few feet inside the foyer."

"Did you see anyone in the hall? Or leaving the building?"

She shook her head again.

"What about since you came back out to the parking lot?" he asked. "Has anyone come outside this way?"

She glanced nervously around the parking lot. "No..."

There was more than one exit, so it was possible that she wouldn't have seen them leaving. But it was also possible that the person who'd messed with her stuff was still inside her place or at least inside the building. Waiting for her to come back?

"You stay here," he advised. "I'll go inside and make sure it's safe." When he turned to head toward the building, she grabbed his arm.

"I locked the door behind me," she said. "You'll need the key." And she held out her ring of keys.

"I have a master key that opens all the doors of the college-owned properties," he said.

Another tremor passed through her so forcefully that she dropped the key ring onto the pavement. He leaned down and picked them up and pressed them into her palm. He must have left his gloves in Dean's office, and maybe she'd left hers in her apartment because her hand was cold. Despite the contact with the coldness of her skin, a flash of heat passed through him. Maybe it was just adrenaline from running here or maybe it was because she was back in Eagle Valley, and he thought he might finally get the truth out of her. But he had to make sure nothing happened to her first.

"You should get in your car and start it up, stay warm…and safe." But if the person who'd messed with her stuff had intended to attack her, they'd already had the opportunity and hadn't taken it. Unless they were waiting to try again, if not in her apartment then somewhere inside the building.

When he turned away from her, she didn't stop him this time. Maybe she saw the gun he was reaching for and knew he would be safe. Would *she*? He wasn't sure if she would do as he'd advised and lock herself inside her vehicle. Perhaps he should have made certain that she did, but he also wanted to be able to catch her intruder if they were still inside her place.

Once he opened the door to her unit, he understood why she'd called for help. All but one of the boxes were trampled, her belongings strewn all over the hardwood floor. Then he noticed the note on the mirror, scrawled across it in thick marker. His pulse quickened, not with fear, but with excitement. There was only one reason why someone wouldn't want her to return to Eagle Valley and St. Michel's: they were afraid of the truth coming out.

And that meant he was right, that he'd been right all this time.

She knew the truth.

She had no idea what to think.

He had a master key, so he could have gotten into

her place even if she hadn't left the door partially open while she was moving. But why would he have trampled her boxes and written that note? She was sure he was the man who'd been calling her relatives trying to locate her. So he should have been happy that she was back.

He certainly hadn't seemed surprised to find her in the parking lot. Obviously he'd been aware that she was coming to St. Michel's. Maybe he'd even orchestrated it. Mara had told her that her brother and Dean Stolz were good friends.

The sudden urge to run overwhelmed her. She grasped the keys so tightly, the metal bit into her palm. But where would she go? And how? She didn't have any cash or credit cards on her.

While she had, fortunately, had her cell phone in her pocket, she'd left her purse inside the apartment. Had the intruder tossed out the contents of that, like the boxes, or had he stolen it? She needed to go back inside, to take inventory of what was missing and what was damaged.

Ryder would require that for his report if he truly was campus security. And he probably was because it would make no sense for him to lie about something she could easily confirm. Just as it made no sense for her to have lied about Skip Holdren's alibi.

But Ryder hadn't believed her ten years ago. And she doubted he would have kept looking for her if he'd accepted that she'd told the truth. Maybe her being back here, the break-in, was all some manipulation on his part to get her to say what he, for some reason, wanted to hear.

Her pulse pounded as fast and hard as it had when she'd found her belongings tossed about her new apartment and had wondered if the intruder was still inside. The real threat might be in her place right now: Ryder Lewis.

She wanted to follow her instinct to run, but, as the child of missionaries, she was too by-the-book to drive without her license. So she shoved the ring of keys back in her pocket, but then she turned away from the apartment building and headed off to the place where she'd always run before when she had needed peace or guidance. The light in the steeple guided her down the brick path toward the church.

But the farther she got away from the parking lot, the less light illuminated her way, casting shadows across the walk and all around Kristy. "This was stupid," she murmured aloud. It would have been smarter to wait for Ryder inside her car with the doors locked like he'd advised.

She had no idea if the vandal was still in her apartment. Or out here…

If they were inside, she wasn't that worried about Ryder. She'd noticed the holster beneath his open jacket—the tan suede one with the sheepskin lining—and he'd been wearing the black cowboy hat.

He had been the rider on the horse she'd seen when she'd first driven onto the campus. But even after seeing him then, she'd still been stunned when he'd showed up in the parking lot. Not as much by his appearance as by what had happened in her apartment: the ransacking, the note…

*You shouldn't have come back!*

While she wholeheartedly agreed, it was too late now. She was here. She'd committed to this adjunct teaching position, and she was going to make the most of it and the most of coming back here.

For Mara...

The fieldstone church at the end of a long stretch of brick path was farther from the faculty apartment building than she'd realized. Nothing stood on either side of it but trees and shadows. Shadows of the trees?

Or shadows of people?

Was someone out there? Watching her? Waiting to see if she'd heeded the implied threat of that note? Obviously the person wanted her to leave St. Michel's. What would they do when she didn't?

Her heart pounded with fear, and she thought about turning around and heading back to her vehicle. But then she'd have to pass through that long, secluded section again, have to wonder what or who might be hiding in those shadows...

Then the darkness deepened even more, and she anxiously looked around before realizing that she stood in the shadow of that fieldstone church. From a distance it looked small, but up close it was bigger, darker...but for the light glowing through the stained glass windows and radiating like a beacon on a lighthouse from the steeple. She ran up the steps, pushed open one of the double doors and stepped into the light. It wasn't bright, but it was warm and chased away the chill that had settled deep inside her since her arrival.

This was how she'd always felt here—warm and safe. Protected.

She released a shaky breath and walked down the aisle toward the front of the church. Every row of seats was empty, but it was late on a Monday night so she doubted there were any services currently scheduled. When there were, she would try to attend them and find out who was now taking care of the small but special church. The minister who'd been here nine years ago had probably retired. Pastor Howard had already been pretty old when she'd started her first of four years at St. Michel's.

He'd been so sweet to her, so supportive of her, especially after the murder. He'd prayed often with her and for her while she'd prayed for Mara. Tears stung her eyes, and she blinked them back to focus on the front of the church and the beautifully carved cross behind the altar.

Stepping into one of the rows of seats, she settled down to pray. And just as she had ten years ago, she prayed for Mara, hoping she was at peace. Then she prayed for Ryder, wishing he could find peace as well, because she knew he hadn't or he wouldn't be here.

She knew because she wouldn't be here if she'd found peace. Despite all Pastor Howard's prayers, it had eluded her. She wasn't able to forgive herself for how she'd betrayed her best friend. And while Ryder had only talked to her about the intruder, she had no doubt that he had much more to say to her about what he believed was the false alibi she'd provided.

How fervently she wished it was false…

"Oh, Mara," she murmured. "Please forgive me."

Maybe if she could somehow sense that Mara had, then Kristy would be able to finally forgive herself and stop the guilt from consuming her. She squeezed her eyes shut to suppress the rush of tears. And she held her breath to smother the sobs rising up from the back of her throat.

She wasn't sure if she was crying for Mara or for herself, and she wasn't going to indulge any self-pity. She had no right to it. Kristy was alive. And Mara...

The creak of hinges and the sudden slam of one of the double doors startled her. She opened her eyes to darkness. Someone had shut off the church lights.

Had the caretaker or minister not noticed that she was inside? Had they closed up the church for the night? She jumped up from her seat and started edging down the row toward the aisle, but as she did, she caught the faint scrape of shoes against the hardwood floor.

She wasn't alone in the church.

Someone else was here...in the dark. Her skin chilled. Had someone followed her from the apartment? But she'd been so careful. She'd kept peering into the shadows along the path and behind her, and she'd noticed no movement. Surely if someone had followed her, she would have heard footsteps then. So thinking that it must be the new pastor or a custodian, she called out, "Hello? Who's there?"

But nobody answered her even as the sound of footsteps grew louder and closer. She always wanted to believe people had the best intentions. Even after

Mara's murder, she didn't want to see and suspect evil being everywhere, but most especially not here—in the little church where she'd sought solace after that murder. But if the person walking toward her meant her no harm, why hadn't he replied to her?

Fear quickening her pulse, she turned and hurried back down the row of seats toward the other the aisle. Because she had no idea what this person wanted with her....

Was this just another attempt to frighten her?

Or was this going to be an attempt to make her go away forever?

# Chapter Four

*Where did she go?*

Ryder had been inside her apartment building lon-ger than he'd intended to be. He'd made certain no-body was hiding anywhere. But he hadn't wanted to leave her outside by herself for long, even though he hadn't noticed anyone lurking around when he'd found her in the parking lot earlier. Once he'd seen how her things had been ransacked, though, he'd called in the state police to come out and process the apartment for fingerprints.

Because they didn't consider it a priority case, they weren't coming out tonight. So he would have to se-cure the apartment as a crime scene and move Kristy to another one. But first he had to find her. She'd ob-viously ignored his advice to lock herself inside her vehicle because the car was dark and empty, the hood cold to his touch. She hadn't even started it.

So where was she? He hadn't seen her inside the apartment building.

And while a bus did run around the campus, he couldn't imagine her getting on it. To go where? Maybe the lecture hall where she'd been assigned to teach? Her first class was tomorrow, but the place was probably already locked up for the night.

"Kristy?" he called out. "Kristy?"

Was she just hiding from him?

She couldn't seriously believe he had anything to do with that stupid note scrawled across the mirror. He was the one who'd wanted her to come back, and she was smart enough to suspect that. That was why she hadn't been surprised to see him.

"Kristy?"

Snow clung to the ground in some places, but the pavement and brick sidewalks were all dry, leaving no trace of her footprints, no indication of where she had gone. So he forced himself to think of his sister, of the texts and emails she'd sent telling him about her roommate and friend.

*She's so sweet.*

*She's so spiritual. Must come from being the kid of missionaries.*

*She spends more time in the little campus church than our apartment.*

After what had happened, how Mara had died after a wild party that her roommate had supposedly never left, Ryder had figured that Mara must had lied about Kristy Kendall. She'd probably told him Kristy was sweet and straitlaced because she'd known how overprotective Ryder tended to be. Loving him like she had, she hadn't wanted him to worry about her, so she'd misled him about Kristy. Just as she'd withheld the truth about her boyfriend and those letters and texts he'd found after she'd died.

After it had been too late for Ryder to save her.

But maybe everything Mara had told him about Kristy hadn't been a lie, so he headed off in the direction of the church. He would at least check to see if she was there. Because Pastor Howard had undoubtedly left it unlocked like he usually did, she would have been able to get inside the church. The old man claimed it was because he wanted everyone to be able to use it when they needed it, but Ryder wondered if the pastor was getting forgetful. Every time Ryder had tried talking to him about Mara or Kristy, he'd claimed he didn't remember them.

How was that possible when the murder of Mara Lewis had become a legend on campus, almost to the level of urban myth? Some people claimed her ghost haunted the apartment building where she died and, despite there being no other murders, some even claimed that her murderer still hunts for victims on the campus, killing hapless sorority girls.

But Mara's murder was the only one, and Ryder hoped to keep it that way. What did the note on Kristy's mirror mean? Was it a threat that something was going to happen to her because she'd returned and shouldn't have?

He hurried up, his cowboy boots stomping against the brick pavers of the walk. As he neared the church, he slowed his pace. Why was it so dark?

As well as leaving it unlocked, Pastor Howard usually left on the lights, too. The darkness made Ryder uneasy even before he heard the scream. And for a moment he was propelled into the past...to when he was a kid who'd witnessed a murder. His mother's murder during a carjacking. At six years old, he had been helpless to save her. Just as he'd been helpless to save Mara.

But this wasn't either of their screams. They were gone. This had to be Kristy. Had her intruder followed her into the church?

He ran up the steps and pushed open one of the double doors. "Kristy?" he called out, his voice gruff with the fear gripping him. He shouldn't have left her alone outside. But his staff was stretched so thin already.

"Kristy?"

He could see nothing in the darkness. But then something passed him, brushing against him. He reached out to grab it, but the shadow slipped away. Then the doors crashed open, and the shadow ran out.

"Kristy?" Was it her? Was she running away from him? He'd suspected she would if she'd realized he was the reason she was here. He started after the shadow, but then a faint whisper in the dark stopped him.

"Ryder?" Her voice came from inside the church, somewhere farther down the aisle.

Lights flickered on, illuminating the small church. Ryder peered around until he spied her, lying on the floor between two rows of seats. His heart hammering with concern, he rushed over and crouched beside her. "Are you okay? What happened? Were you attacked?"

She rolled over and peered up at him, with her brow furrowed and eyes squinted as if she couldn't see him. Her glasses were missing, so maybe she couldn't.

"Are you okay?" he asked again. "Were you hurt?"

She patted the floor and came up with those tortoiseshell frames. Her breath escaped in a sigh of relief and she slid them on before sitting up. "I'm okay," she said. "I don't know what happened. The lights went off…"

"That happens sometimes," a man said as he walked down the aisle toward them.

Pastor Howard wore his customary all black, but for the tiny bit of white collar showing at the base of his neck. If he'd been the one who'd passed Ryder and rushed out of the church, why hadn't he said anything?

"How did the lights come back on?" Ryder asked.

The older man smiled. "I threw the breaker in the basement. Something must have tripped it off, but with this old wiring, it could have been anything."

Ryder suspected it had been a human. And with concern he turned toward the one he crouched beside. Most of her thick, silky, chocolate-brown hair had escaped from her bun, falling down over her shoulders and her back. "Did you see anyone? How did you wind up on the floor? Were you pushed?"

She shook her head. "The lights going off scared me," she admitted. "And then I heard someone coming down the aisle and tried to get away…"

"Had they grabbed you?" Ryder asked, his stomach muscles tightening with dread and guilt for leaving her unprotected. He'd been so focused on finding out who'd killed his sister that he didn't realize Kristy's return could put her in danger—that *he* could have put her in danger—and his stomach churned knowing that he had done that.

She shook her head again. "I tripped and fell and lost my glasses and…" Tears shimmered for a moment in her dark eyes, but she blinked them back and looked over his shoulder at the man who'd come up behind him. "Pastor Howard…you're still here."

"Miss Kendall," the older man remarked, his voice warm with delight. "I heard you were coming back to our campus. It's so wonderful to see you again."

Ryder glanced back at the older man. "I thought you didn't remember who she was."

The older man blinked at him as if confused. And maybe he was. "Of course I remember Miss Kendall. She and I spent a lot of time together." He stepped around Ryder and reached out to help Kristy to her feet. Despite his age, the man was strong and spry and far more chivalrous than Ryder had been.

But that scream had rattled Ryder so much, had sent him reeling back into the past, into his worst nightmares—which was what Mara's murder had done.

"I didn't know if you'd still be here," she said, and she smiled widely before hugging the pastor. "I'm so glad."

"And I'm so happy you've returned."

"How did you know I was coming back?" she asked.

Ryder wondered himself.

"The school newsletter announced it, and Dean Stolz posted it on the college website as well to encourage students to sign up for your creative writing course," he said. "I am tempted to sign up myself. You are such a talented author. Thank you so much for sending me that autographed copy of your book. I enjoyed it immensely."

Kristy chuckled. "Then you were one of the few."

While Ryder was aware she had a publishing credit for an article or two, he hadn't realized she'd had a book published as well. But Dean probably wouldn't have hired her if she'd just had the articles on her CV, even as a favor to him.

Ryder studied her now, wondering what she was really like. The image he'd had in his head all these years of the wild party girl, or the good girl Mara had claimed she was?

"Your book was wonderful," the pastor assured her. "Just as I knew it would be."

They had clearly been close, aligning more with what Mara had told Ryder about her roommate. But why had the pastor lied about remembering her?

And what else might he be lying about? Focused on what had just happened, on what had made her scream, Ryder redirected the conversation. "Were you in the church when the lights went off?"

The pastor turned toward Ryder with that confused look on his face again, his forehead furrowed beneath wisps of white hair. "The lights went off?"

"Yes, you just said that you turned the breaker back on," he reminded him.

"Oh, that happens all the time."

Ryder wasn't certain that was what had happened tonight. He focused on Kristy. "You said you heard someone coming toward you in the dark?" It must have been whoever had rushed out of the church when he'd been coming in.

She nodded. "I could hear their footsteps, but I called to them and they didn't reply. They just kept coming." Her voice shook like her body had earlier.

The pastor sighed. "I'm sorry, Kristy. My hearing isn't what it used to be. I probably didn't hear you."

"I wasn't calling out that loudly," she ruefully admitted.

"I heard you scream," Ryder said. And he remembered again those quick seconds at the stoplight, the broken window, his mother's scream and the shot...

It had all happened so quickly. He hadn't been able to do anything then.

The pastor shook his head. "I didn't. I must have been downstairs turning the breaker back on then."

So he couldn't have been the person who'd run out of the church. Whom had that been? And what was going on?

"Why did you scream?" Ryder asked her.

"Because I fell, and I wasn't sure what I tripped over."

"A person?"

"I don't know," she said. "I think I'm just freaked out after what happened earlier."

"What was that, dear?" the pastor asked. "Are you all right?"

She nodded. "I'm fine."

But Ryder suspected she was lying, just like she'd lied about Skip Holdren's alibi. She had to be because he was certain Skip was Mara's killer. "I need to talk to Kristy some more about that earlier incident," Ryder said.

"What was that?" the pastor asked again.

Ryder opened his mouth, but before he could say anything, Kristy replied first, "Nothing serious, Pastor. But I should go back to my apartment with Mr. Lewis right now. You and I will catch up another time."

Pastor Howard nodded his gray-haired head. "I am sure I will be seeing you here like I used to."

She smiled at him, but she didn't confirm or deny his assumption. Was she even going to stay in Eagle Valley after what had happened? Or was she going to disappear again like Ryder had been afraid she already had when he'd returned to the parking lot and hadn't been able to find her?

He couldn't help but wonder if it would be smarter and safer for both of them if she didn't stay.

All the way back to the faculty apartment building, Kristy had that same sensation that she'd had earlier—that fear and suspicion that someone was lurking in the dark shadows along the brick path watching her.

Watching *them* now.

She should have been reassured that she wasn't alone, but despite his being with campus security, Ryder Lewis unsettled and frightened her. Was that his intent?

Did he want to scare her?

"You're really a security guard?" she asked skeptically. Hearing the squeaky nerves in her voice, she winced.

"No," he replied.

She tensed and stopped walking, wishing now that she'd demanded proof when he'd first told her that he was. They had already made it to the parking lot, though, with her nearly jogging to keep up with his long strides. "But you said—"

"I'm head of campus security," he said.

"I thought you were a rodeo rider," she said.

He shook his head. "Not anymore." He started up the steps to the building.

She wanted to ask him why he'd given it up, but she had a feeling she knew: Mara. Or more specifically, Mara's unsolved murder. "Apparently Dean Stolz doesn't worry about someone's credentials for a position," she murmured as she followed him and stepped through the door he held open for her that led to the foyer.

"Are you talking about me or you?" Ryder asked, his deep voice gruff.

She couldn't tell if he was angry with her or not. At Mara's memorial, she'd had no doubt that he was. "I think we both know why I'm here."

"You wrote a book," he said.

She snorted. "One book," she said. "And it's not *Catcher in the Rye*, and I'm no JD Salinger."

"Shhh," he said. "I won't tell Dean if you don't." He focused on her then, and there was no mistaking the cold anger in his blue eyes. "I know you're good at keeping secrets."

She shook her head in denial. "I have no secrets," she said. "Dean is fully aware of my qualifications." Pitiful though they were. But she knew he wasn't talking about her resume; he was talking about Skip Holdren's alibi. *Her*...

"He's aware of mine, too," Ryder said. "That after we went through boot camp together, I served as an MP with the US Marine Corp. And between deployments, and later downtime in the rodeo, I got a degree in criminal justice."

"Justice," she whispered. That was why he was here; she had no doubt about that. He wanted justice for his sister's murder, which was why he'd orchestrated her return. He thought she could help him get it.

If only she could....

But she remembered so little from that night. It was just the next morning that was burned so vividly into her mind. She didn't even have to close her eyes to see Mara.

"I checked out your apartment," he said, as if he hadn't heard what she'd murmured. And maybe he hadn't. "I didn't find anyone inside."

She released a shaky breath and headed up the stairs to the second floor. His boots echoed her shoes on the treads. Once on the landing, she rushed down the hall toward her apartment door, pulling the key from her pocket. "If it's safe, it's not necessary for you to come in," she said when he stopped beside her outside her apartment.

"I need to take a full report from you. You have to give me an inventory of everything that's missing or damaged," he said.

She was.

Ever since that day she'd found Mara, Kristy had felt like she was lost...missing and damaged.

## Chapter Five

A pang struck Ryder's heart over the look on her face. She suddenly seemed so lost and frightened. So young.

Like Mara had been.

His younger sister had been just twenty when she'd died...much too soon. Ten years had passed, and since she and her roommate had been the same age, Kristy would be thirty now. But there were no lines on her face, no color at all now but the faint trace of darkness beneath her eyes as if she hadn't been sleeping well.

Ryder hadn't slept well for ten years, and even before Mara's murder, other nightmares had occasionally interrupted his sleep. He doubted he would even close his eyes tonight. Kristy probably wouldn't either, at least not in that unit. But he wasn't leaving her there, even as he unlocked the door and pushed it open for her. "Be careful to touch as few things as you can," he said. "But let me know if you notice anything missing."

She passed in front of him to step inside the foyer,

and her gaze immediately went to the mirror—to that message scrawled across the glass. The letters were block-like, so the writer had disguised their handwriting. They probably had worn gloves, as well, but hopefully the state police techs would find something when they processed the scene.

"I left my purse on the kitchen counter when I went back for the last of my things," she said. That was probably the box that was still packed and standing uncrumpled where she must have dropped it, just inside the door. She walked past it and stepped over the upended boxes and belongings to slip through the doorway to the small, galley kitchen. "My purse is here," she said. "It doesn't look like it was touched."

He, likewise, stepped over the scattered things to join her in the small kitchen with its clean but outdated oak cabinets and white countertops. "No cash or credit cards missing?" he asked.

She peered inside her wallet and shook her head. "No."

"Then it wasn't a theft…unless there's something else missing. Did you have anything valuable in the boxes?"

She tried to move around him to pass through the doorway, but there wasn't much space between the sides of the galley kitchen. And as she brushed against him, her breath audibly caught. His did, too, as a sudden awareness gripped him. With all that long, silky-looking brown hair, creamy skin and big, thickly-lashed dark eyes, Kristy Kendall was more beautiful than he remembered.

Not that he was attracted to her.

The only interest he had in her was in getting her to admit the truth. And keeping her safe while she was here.

She quickly moved away from him and focused on the items spilled out of the boxes. "I didn't have much in these boxes but clothes and books. That last box…that's my go-box," she said.

"Go-box?" he queried. "What's that?"

"Something my parents taught me to always have packed in case we had to leave a village or an area quickly, in case there was danger…"

"What kind of danger?" he asked, curious about her life.

She shrugged. "I wasn't sure then. My parents tried to shelter me. But I learned later that the times we left a village in the middle of the night was because of an insurrection or a kidnapping threat. Missionaries are sometimes taken hostage."

He sucked in a breath, fearful of what she'd been through, of the risks missionaries took in order to help other people. "Were you ever…"

She shook her head. "No, nothing ever happened to us. But I did have to leave some things behind before and do without for a while. So I make certain I have the essentials and necessities packed." She pointed toward the unopened box. "My laptop is in there, along with enough clothes and toiletries for a week."

He stepped around her and picked it up. "We'll bring this to a vacant apartment down the hall."

"There's another vacancy?" she asked.

"There are several," he said. "St. Michel's doesn't get many adjunct professors in the spring. They're usually here in the fall, and many of them stay in Eagle Valley. The town has grown a lot over the past decade," he said. "There are more shops and restaurants and a few housing developments. Most of the professors live there."

"What about you?" she asked. "Where do you live?"

Her petite body tensed as if she was afraid he might say he lived in this building where she was staying. A smile tugged at his lips, and he replied, "I have my own place on campus near the stable." It was actually attached to the stable through the tack room. It wasn't much, but then, he didn't spend a lot of time there anyway.

Her body relaxed a bit, as if relieved by his answer.

"But I'm going to stay here tonight," he said. "To make sure nothing gets disturbed."

"You really think someone might come back?" she asked, and she shuddered as she peered around the place.

"I don't know," he said. "You're still here." He juggled the box in one arm to pull open the door to the hall.

She hurried out past him as if she couldn't wait to leave. He closed the door behind them and led the way a short distance down the hall to another apartment he unlocked. He pushed open that door for her to precede him.

"Once the state police process the other apartment,

you can get the rest of your stuff and move it here, or stay there if you'd like," Ryder told her.

She nodded as she looked around at the unit that was identical, in dated decor and furnishings, to the one she'd originally been assigned. Everything was the same, but here there was no mess, no note scrawled across the mirror.

"Are you going to stay?" he wondered aloud. Or had that message or his presence scared her off?

"In that apartment or on campus?" she asked.

"On campus," he clarified.

"I agreed to teach the entire semester," she said. "I'm staying."

Since hearing her scream, or maybe even since her call to dispatch, he'd had a heavy pressure on his chest. And it didn't ease with relief that she wasn't leaving, like he'd expected it to; instead, it seemed to grow heavier with the fear that her presence might have put her in danger. "I'm not sure if that's a good thing or not," he admitted.

"If you had an agenda for getting Dean to hire me, you wasted your time," she said. "I don't know any more about Mara's murder than I knew ten years ago."

He shook his head, but he wasn't denying being behind her job offer, just her claim. "If that was the case, that message wouldn't have been scrawled on the mirror. I'm obviously not the only one who thinks you know more than you're admitting."

"But who and why? Who else could be as wrong about that as you are?"

He narrowed his eyes in irritation. "The killer," he

said. "He could be worried that you're going to finally tell the truth, and he'll lose his alibi."

"Skip Holdren did not kill your sister, and I don't know why you're so convinced that he did. And I doubt he has any idea I've come back to St. Michel's, not that he would care." Her face flushed with color then, as if she was embarrassed.

"He didn't fall in love with you like you wanted?" he asked. He wasn't able to find proof that Skip, or his wealthy parents, had paid her for that alibi, so she had to have lied for him because she'd been obsessed with him, just like he'd been obsessed with Mara. Ryder had seen the texts Skip had sent Mara when he'd pulled her cell phone records. He'd also read all the love letters from the guy to Mara, all the promises and then the threats when she'd refused to take their relationship beyond the innocent dating they'd done. Skip had sounded obsessed and then unhinged, so Ryder had no doubt Mara's boyfriend had murdered her. No one else she'd known had had a motive to kill her, and with no sign of forced entry, she must have let in her killer. She'd been too smart to let a stranger into her apartment.

"I was not in love with Skip," she said. "And like I said, I doubt he even knows I'm here."

"He lives on his parents' estate, and he would have received the college newsletter, and maybe he saw the notice Dean put on the website about your teaching here," Ryder pointed out. He hadn't realized his friend had done that or considered the risk that might pose to Kristy. He was definitely going to stick close to her since her return for a couple of reasons: to get her to admit the truth and to make sure that nobody tried to hurt her.

He'd already lost too many women he'd cared about. Not that he cared about Kristy. He didn't even really know her, but that was good. He knew what he had to know about her: she was lying.

But even if she wasn't a liar, he wouldn't have been tempted to care for her. He'd vowed long enough to never get involved like that, to never risk that kind of loss again. He'd already suffered enough heartbreak.

She shrugged. "Then a lot of other people were able to learn that I was coming here, too," she said.

"So there's someone else that might not have wanted you to return?" he asked. "Or maybe someone who didn't want you to leave where you were? A boyfriend you left behind?" His breath caught in his throat with that question, along with some strange little pang in his heart.

Her lips curved into a slight wistful smile. "No boyfriend."

That breath he'd drawn in escaped in a soft sigh. "Then it has to be *someone here* who doesn't think you should have come back."

She shrugged again. "I have no idea who that could be. I just know that Skip has no reason to threaten me. I can't hurt him or anyone else because I have already told everyone the truth about what I remember from Mara's murder."

She sounded sincere, so sincere that Ryder might have started to believe her if not for the threat she'd been left. And had the breaker really gone off on its own at the church? Or had someone thrown that switch in order to get her in the dark? And do what?

Just how much danger was Kristy Kendall in over returning to St. Michel's campus? Another twinge struck Ryder's heart, this time easily identifiable as guilt. He'd wanted to solve his sister's murder, not cause another one.

Kristy probably wouldn't have slept well the night before even if her boxes hadn't been ransacked and Ryder Lewis hadn't shown up to investigate.

She would have been too nervous over teaching her first class to sleep. When Dean Stolz had extended the offer to her, she'd worked hard on lesson plans that followed the curriculum guidelines he'd given her. Having gotten her master's degree after graduating from St. Michel's, it seemed as if she'd never stopped learning, and she'd even worked as a TA in graduate school, working toward her doctorate. Mostly, she'd just led study groups. She'd probably done more actual teaching when she'd helped her parents with the kids in the missionary schools, but she'd never taught a class on her own before.

And these students who were rich and smart enough to get into the exclusive private college were nothing like those children in the third-world countries where Kristy's parents had served as missionaries.

Standing at the podium in front of a lecture hall frightened her almost as much as the events of the previous evening had. The way the students stared at her felt threatening. Not that there were many of them; there were far more empty seats in the lecture hall than filled ones. But then, she probably wasn't much of a draw for a creative writing course. Prospective students would prefer to learn from someone who had written a bestselling novel or a screenplay that had been made into a movie or television series. She'd done nothing that impressive; she'd just written a memoir about her life growing up as the kid of missionaries.

The longer she stood there, silently, the harder these college students stared at her. The more they judged her and found her lacking, just like Ryder had judged her all those years ago when he'd lashed out at her at Mara's memorial service.

And last night...

Even after what had happened, or maybe because of it, he had seemed even more convinced that she was lying. That she was a fraud.

Her face heated with embarrassment because she was pretty sure all these students thought she was one, too. If only these kids were like the children from those remote villages and undeveloped islands...

If only they were that eager to learn, that hungry for knowledge...

"I don't know why you're all here," she finally began, her voice scratchy with nerves. "I'm not even sure why I'm here."

But she was pretty certain that Ryder Lewis was behind that job offer.

Now that she was here, though, she was going to make the most of it.

There were murmurs within the lecture hall, grumbling. A couple students even stood up as if they intended to leave.

"But I remember why I wanted to write—why I wanted to share my stories with the world."

Some of the students perked up, leaned forward, as she slowly drew the interest of at least a few of them. Nobody reminded her yet of the kids from the missionary schools. They weren't that eager to learn, that enthralled.

They were just curious about the reasons someone else would want to write. But she could work with curiosity.

So she continued. "I'm the daughter of a couple of missionaries who travel all around the world, teaching kids who would have no formal schooling without them. These children, some of them midteens, had no idea what a TV is, let alone a cell phone…and when I told them about all the material things that I had in the United States, it was as if I was spinning fairy tales to them. They couldn't believe such devices existed, and so I learned to describe things to them that they'd never seen before, never touched, never used—things they wouldn't have even been able to dream of—and after I described it to them, they could dream."

The students who'd stood up, as if to head toward the exit, took their seats again. Seeing that she had a few more of them interested in what she was saying, she stepped out from behind the podium and walked up to the first row. "That's what a writer should do—make the reader be able to picture everything so vividly in the story that it sticks with them, that they dream about it."

Like she'd dreamed about Mara again last night. And Ryder…

But instead of yelling at her and being angry with her, Ryder had been protecting her. But from what?

Who had scrawled that threat on her mirror?

And why?

Why would someone not want her back at St. Michel's?

She forced those thoughts from her mind as she focused on her class, on drawing them in with her words like she'd once drawn in those children her parents had helped. But these kids weren't as innocent as those children had been.

They asked her more questions about the financial benefits of writing than about the mechanics of crafting a story. They wanted to know how much they could expect to make off their stories. She sidestepped those questions and redirected them to remember why they wanted to write, about the passion of storytelling…even if no one listened.

Just as Ryder didn't seem to listen when she told him over and over again that she hadn't lied. She'd been thinking about him so much that she must have conjured him up, because she caught a glimpse of him slipping out the door after class. He'd been here?

To monitor her class or her?

To protect her or threaten her?

# Chapter Six

She'd probably seen him. Ryder hadn't snuck out of the lecture hall as quickly as he'd wanted. He'd been too surprised, by how fascinating her first lesson had been, to move as fast as he normally would have. Or maybe he was too tired from not sleeping the night before. He'd been on edge, listening to see if anyone was trying to break into her place again. Because he'd been so worried about her, he'd decided to attend her class to keep an eye on her.

Dean had also sat in on it, and Ryder followed the provost back to his office to find out why. While Dean dropped into the chair behind his desk, Ryder remained standing near the door that opened onto the reception area. He didn't have time to stay; he had to check with the state police to see if they'd found anything in Kristy's originally assigned apartment. And he had to make sure that she stayed safe as well.

"Not like you to take time out of your busy schedule to sit in on the first class of a new adjunct professor," Ryder remarked.

Dean leaned back and chuckled. "Not like you to ever sit in on a class of any professor… At least, not since you got your criminal justice degree. What were you doing there today? Or do I even have to ask?"

"I had my reasons," Ryder said, and he moved closer to Dean's desk before lowering his voice to add, "And my concerns." About her safety after what had happened the night before. He needed to bring the provost up to speed on the events of the previous evening.

"I had my concerns, too," Dean admitted, "that this might have been a mistake—that she might not be able to engage the students."

Ryder expelled a soft breath of awe over how well she'd done. "That wasn't the case."

"She started out—no, she didn't start out at all," Dean said. "She just stood up there for the longest time, and I thought I was going to have to step in and rescue her. But she pulled it off. And she handled the students brilliantly, getting them interested while fielding their more personal questions."

About money. She'd acted as if it really didn't matter to her. Was that because she had money coming in from Skip Holdren? Had he paid her for his alibi? Ryder hadn't found any proof of it ten years ago, and he didn't see any now either.

From the condition of her vehicle and the modest belongings that had been strewn around her apartment, he doubted she'd taken a bribe. So maybe Skip had somehow convinced her that she was telling the truth. Because she seemed to think she was, or at least that was what she wanted Ryder to believe.

And he wanted to believe her. Because there was something about her…something that drew his interest.

He had been just as enthralled as those students during her lesson. He'd hung on her every word like they had. She was a good teacher. And because of that, because she'd been Mara's friend, Ryder wanted her to be a good person as well.

Not that anything could ever come of his interest in her. He'd already lost too many women he'd cared about to risk caring about anyone else. First his mom, and then Mara, who'd been his half sister. She was the daughter of his stepmother, who his dad had married a few years after Ryder's mother's senseless murder. She'd died in a carjacking when Ryder had been just a kid.

Ryder drew in as deep a breath as he could with that heavy pressure still sitting on his chest. "I'm beginning to think it was a mistake to bring her here," he admitted.

Dean's mouth fell open, and he leaned back in his chair, clearly shocked. "What the…" He shook his head. "You badgered me for years to do this, to extend that job offer to her and get her to come back to Eagle Valley, and now you're having second thoughts?"

"Yes," Ryder said. "Someone got into her place last night—"

"Broke in?"

He shook his head. "She was moving stuff in and had left the doors propped open. Someone took advantage of that to toss her stuff around and smash her boxes."

Dean snorted. "Probably some frat boys playing a prank."

"There was a message scrawled across the mirror on the foyer wall saying she shouldn't have come back."

Dean leaned forward. "Isn't that vindication for you? Proof that you've been right about her?"

"That's what I thought at first," Ryder admitted. "But she seems so sincere…"

"Maybe she is," Dean said. "And as hard for you to admit as it might be, you could have been wrong all these years."

Panic clenched his heart at the thought. But then he remembered those letters and texts Skip had sent his sister. They could have been used in court to show his motive, but the alibi had assured that no case was ever brought against him. He'd never even been thoroughly investigated because Kristy had sworn she'd been with him that night.

But even more than those letters and texts, Ryder had his instincts, and every single one of them had screamed at him, even louder than Kristy had screamed in the dark church last night, that he was right.

"Doesn't matter why you wanted me to hire her. I'm just happy you talked me into it," Dean admitted. "Doing you this favor is going to turn out well for me, too." And his lips curved into an almost wolfish grin with dimples piercing his cheeks.

Ryder felt that twinge again, the one he'd felt when he'd asked Kristy about ex-boyfriends, and this time he realized it was jealousy. Was his friend interested in her? He'd just recently gone through a divorce. Was he looking to start dating again?

Ryder couldn't remember the last time he, himself, had gone out on a date. Certainly not since he'd accepted his new position as the head of campus security. There was always something to do to occupy his time but never, completely, his mind. Thoughts of justice always monopolized his mind. And thoughts of Kristy...

But it was just as well that he had no time for dating. He'd lost the women he'd cared most about in the world to violence, and he knew, all too well, that he couldn't protect them or himself from that kind of pain. But with Kristy he wasn't too late to try to save her.

"I think it was a mistake," he said. "I think you should rescind your offer and make her leave the campus immediately."

A gasp drew his attention to the door he'd left open, and he saw Kristy standing just outside the provost's office. Her face flushed a bright, red either with anger over his wanting her fired or with embarrassment that she'd been caught eavesdropping. But instead of staying to let him explain, she turned and rushed through the reception area and out into the hall.

She'd expected the provost to sit in on her class; he'd even warned her that he would monitor it. But she hadn't expected to see Ryder. Fortunately she hadn't noticed either of them until they'd gotten up and walked out, or she would have been too rattled, too nervous to speak as easily as she, eventually, had to her students.

Once she'd seen Ryder and Dean leave, she'd hurried out after them despite the students trying to fire more questions at her. She'd promised to answer all those questions during her next class.

But after overhearing what she just had, would there be a next class?

By his own admission, that she'd shamelessly eavesdropped to overhear, Dean had let Ryder coerce him into extending her the job offer. Now Ryder wanted him to rescind it. Would the provost let his old friend convince him to do that as well?

After what had happened the night before, how frightened she'd been, she should have been relieved that she might be released from her contract. But, after she'd gotten over her initial nerves, she'd enjoyed teaching. And there was something about being back here, where her best friend had died, that made her feel closer to Mara again, that made her feel as if her old friend would have forgiven her...even though Kristy couldn't forgive herself.

And she had no illusion now that Ryder would ever forgive her either. Not that she expected or wanted him to. She had only hoped that he would someday come to accept that she spoke the truth, that she wasn't helping Mara's murderer elude justice.

At the moment, she just wanted to elude Ryder.

The minute he'd realized she'd overheard his conversation, he'd looked as horrified as she'd felt. Not wanting to deal with the embarrassment burning her up over being caught eavesdropping, she'd turned and run out of the reception area and into the hall of the administration building.

Fortunately there was a long break between classes, so the hallway was full of faculty between assignments and students who were either seeking advisement or working in the building, which made it easy for her to get lost within the crowd. With as tall as Ryder was and the black cowboy hat he wore, he would never blend in and was easy to track with a glance back over her shoulder.

The provost's office was on the top floor of the administration building with no elevators, so she headed toward the stairwell at the end of the hall. Not as many people were within the smaller space, but there were enough that she was elbow to elbow with other people descending the steps.

Until suddenly a hand touched her, pressing hard against her back, pushing her through the people until she lost her footing and fell.

# Chapter Seven

So much for being head of security when he hadn't even noticed the person standing outside the open door of the provost's office until she'd gasped and whirled away. He rushed out after her, but he wasn't alone. Dean moved as fast as she had.

"I'll talk to her," he told his old friend as they nearly collided in the narrow doorway on their way out.

But Dean shook his head and continued through the reception area of his office. "I want to make sure she knows that *I* don't want her to leave."

Ryder didn't want her to leave either. But staying might put her in danger.

And maybe she wasn't the only one. He felt threatened as well, or at least the things he'd believed for so long were at risk. He had to accept that he might have been wrong about Kristy Kendall and his sister's killer. That realization, after all the years of being so certain, scared him.

At the moment though, he was most afraid for her

and had to make sure she was okay. Dean had already beat him through the reception area, but Ryder quickly followed him out. There was a crowd in the hall, such a big one that it had swallowed first Kristy's petite body and then Dean got absorbed into it, too. Ryder tried to peer over people's heads and determine where she'd gone.

He cared less about finding the provost. Dean had probably been stopped, as he usually was, with faculty and students clamoring for his attention, like those students had gathered around Kristy for hers after her class ended. He'd figured she would have stayed there and stayed safe with the number of people and potential witnesses around. But she'd left the lecture hall.

She must have been seeking out Dean. And now Dean was looking for her. But Ryder was determined to find her first, to explain why he wanted her gone.

For her own protection.

He stopped in the middle of the hallway and turned to look over everyone's heads in both directions. He didn't see that pileup of rich brown hair fighting free of a loose bun on top of a head. But he noticed the door to one of the stairwells open and close and open and close again. Of course she would have gone down to the main level, as anxious as she'd been to get away.

From him.

Although she probably hadn't wanted to talk to Dean either and give him a chance to let her go like Ryder had urged him to do. Hopefully she'd also overheard the part where Dean had expressed delight in how well she'd done teaching her first class, with how she'd engaged the students and inspired them.

Ryder hadn't wanted to hurt her feelings; he just wanted to keep her safe. And in order to do that, he needed to find her. There were two stairwells—one at either end of the hall. The stairwell farther away was closer to the parking lot; the other one was closer to Dean's office.

He cut through the people toward that one. It wasn't used as much as the stairwell near the parking lot, but when he stepped inside, he found it crowded with people. They weren't moving; they were standing, staring at the bottom of the stairs. Then his phone began to vibrate within his pocket, and he knew...

"The campus cowboy cop is here," a student remarked.

"That was fast." A woman held up her cell phone. "I just called."

"What happened?" he asked, but he was already weaving through them toward the stairs. And as he looked down, he saw her.

Most of her brown hair had escaped that bun to pool on the floor around her head. She was sprawled facedown across the landing. Dean crouched beside her.

"What happened?" he asked his friend, his voice hoarse with the emotions rushing up on him.

Dean shrugged. "I don't know. She must have slipped and fallen."

Because she'd been in such a hurry to get away from him; this was his fault. That pressure on his chest was so heavy now that it felt as if it was going to crush his heart. *Please, God, let her be all right.*

She looked so limp and lifeless lying there. Was he too late? Just as he'd been with other women he'd cared about.

"She has a pulse," Dean said, his fingers wrapped around her delicate wrist. "But I didn't want to move her."

"Don't," Ryder told him as he dropped to his knees beside her crumpled body. "She could have serious injuries."

For his training to become an MP with the Marines, Ryder had been required to learn first aid. And he'd used it often during his deployment, and it had also come in handy during his rodeo days. He'd had to rush to the aide of his riding buddies several times to quickly assess the seriousness of their injuries before moving them out of the way of the hooves of a scared bronc.

He ran his hands gently over Kristy, hoping that he would find no broken bones. Especially not a broken neck.

The odd angle at which she lay made it clear that she'd struck her head. Almost as if she'd fallen headfirst. But how? Had she been going so fast that she'd entirely lost her footing with both feet?

"Kristy?" he called out to her as he swiped the hair back from her face. She didn't move at all, not even so much as a twitch of her eyelid. And her skin was pale except for the blood that trickled from a wound on her forehead. She could have a concussion.

Or worse…

Bleeding on the brain.

She needed medical help now. Or she might never regain consciousness.

Being carried in the strong arms wrapped around her felt a like a dream to Kristy, or maybe more of a memory. But she couldn't remember anyone ever carrying her like this. As a child, whenever her father had carried her, he'd acted like she was an airplane or a sack of potatoes. And it had been a game.

With her giggling and his deep chuckle.

But nobody was laughing now. She heard the low rumble of deep voices. Who was talking?

Where was she?

She tried to open her eyes, but her lids were so heavy she had to fight, had to summon all her strength, just to lift them. And even then, her eyes opened only a fraction, just enough for her to see shadows, blurry shadows.

Was that because it was getting dark? Or because of her vision?

She reached up then, feeling for her glasses, but they weren't on her face. She touched, instead, a cut on her nose, and a little cry of pain slipped out of her lips. The deep voices stopped, and then suddenly a light flashed in her eyes. She flinched and lifted her hand again, trying to block out the light and the pain which pounded hard and insistently inside her skull.

"How do you feel?"

Kristy didn't recognize the male voice; the man

sounded older than Dean and Ryder but not as old as Pastor Howard. "Who are you?" she asked. "And where am I?"

"You're in the campus clinic," the man replied. "I'm Dr. Ivan."

"Doctor..." She opened her eyes wider and tried to see his face, but it was a blur of pale skin fringed with gray hair. Everything else was just a blur to her as she tried to remember what had happened since she'd run out of Dean Stolz's office.

"How do you feel?" he asked again.

She raised her hand to her forehead, and her fingers brushed across a small bandage. She must have gotten a cut, and she definitely had a bump. She flinched as she touched the raised flesh beneath that bandage. "Headache..."

It was more than a headache, though; it was like someone was inside her brain, pounding to get out, trying to smash through her skull.

"You might have that for a while," he said. "You have a concussion. You need to be monitored to determine how serious it is and if you should be transferred to the hospital in Eagle Valley."

Monitored...

Just like Dean and Ryder had monitored her class, sitting in the back of the lecture hall so that she hadn't noticed them. She remembered following them out and over to the administration building.

Then she'd overheard that conversation. Ryder wanting Dean to release her from her contract...

To get rid of her.

"What happened?" she asked, her mouth dry with the fear gripping her. Had they tried to permanently eliminate her?

"You fell down a flight of stairs," Dr. Ivan replied.

She shook her head, then flinched as a wave of pain and dizziness crashed over her. "No..."

And now she remembered.

She remembered the hands on her back, shoving. She had no doubt that sensation had been real—as real as the pounding in her head and the aches in her body. She hadn't slipped and fallen on those stairs; someone had pushed her down them.

Had tried to kill her?

A sudden chill rushed over her, raising goose bumps on her skin. She shivered over the horrible, terrifying thought. Someone wasn't just trying to warn her to leave St. Michel's campus; someone wanted her permanently gone.

Dead.

And she could think of only one reason why: Ryder was right.

She knew more about Mara's murder than she'd realized.

And whatever she knew made her a threat to Mara's killer—a threat they wanted to eliminate.

So if she was smart, she would quit before Dean could fire her, and she would get in her clunker and drive far away from St. Michel's and Eagle Valley, Michigan. And she would never come back.

That thought brought on more chills and a rush of guilt and regret. She'd already failed Mara once.

She couldn't do it again.

If there was any way Kristy could finally get her old friend the justice she'd deserved and been denied all these years, then she had to do it.

Even if it put her own life at risk.

# *Chapter Eight*

Ryder had lost his faith so many years ago. Maybe in the street where the carjacker had tossed his mother's dead body before pulling Ryder out of the back to join her on the pavement. He'd raised the gun to Ryder's head, but he hadn't pulled the trigger. He hadn't released the bullet.

Other people, his dad and a few years later his stepmother, had tried to point out to him that that must have been God's intervention; that God had saved him. But if God had been able to save him, why hadn't He saved Ryder's mother?

Why hadn't he saved Mara?

Why did bad things keep happening to people Ryder cared about?

After leaving Kristy with Dean and Dr. Ivan at the campus clinic, he'd found himself here: at the campus church.

He wasn't sure if he'd come here to pray for her, to ask for God's intervention again, so that she would regain consciousness. Or if he just wanted to ask Him the question that had haunted Ryder for so long.

"Why?" he asked.

Why his mother?

Why Mara?

Why was someone going after Kristy now?

But he knew that just as there were good people in the world, like his mother and Mara, there were bad, and they would do anything to get what they wanted or to get away with what they'd done. And somehow Kristy was the key to exposing one of these bad people, to stopping them from doing anything else to anyone else…if she lived.

"Please, God," he murmured, his hands clasped together as he leaned forward on the church seat. He hadn't prayed in so long that he wasn't sure he remembered how, but he had to try. He needed to ask God for His help, for Kristy. He was praying for her. "Please make sure she's okay."

Before he'd moved her, he'd checked to make sure she had no obviously broken bones. Of course she could have fractures, small breaks, which were undetectable without X-rays. But her neck had been fine, and her back as well, and so he'd gently carried her to the clinic, wanting to make sure that Dr. Ivan was able to assess the severity of her head injury right away.

She had to have a concussion since she hadn't regained consciousness. How severe was it?

Was she awake yet?

Had she been transferred to the hospital for an MRI and CT scan?

He could have stuck around like Dean had, waiting until she woke up or being there in case she didn't. But Ryder had felt too helpless, as he had in the past.

He hadn't been able to save his mother the day she'd died. He hadn't been able to protect Mara either.

And after checking for broken bones, there hadn't been anything else he could have done for Kristy.

But this…

Pray.

He closed his eyes and tried to focus, but the words wouldn't come. He couldn't remember the things he'd been taught in Sunday school. After his mom died, he'd tuned them all out. Now he could think of nothing to say but…

"Please, God, make sure she wakes up and that she's okay."

He couldn't wait to find out if the prayers worked. He had to check on her. The church was quiet, but since he was the only one inside it this early in the morning, he wasn't worried about disturbing that tranquility when he pulled out his cell phone. He scrolled through his call log, expecting that Dean had phoned him from the stairwell, that he would have called Ryder the second he'd found Kristy since he knew about Ryder's first aid training.

But he had no missed calls from his friend.

Maybe Dean had already heard that someone else had called for the "campus cowboy cop." Ryder knew the students called him that, but he didn't mind. The cowboy hat and the boots somehow made him more approachable to them. They had no problem letting him know where drugs were being dealt or under-age drinking took place. They seemed to get a kick out of him riding in on Sable to break up the parties.

He was glad they felt comfortable enough to speak freely with him, to come to him when they knew there was going to be trouble. If only he'd made Kristy feel that safe.

But instead he was the one who'd put her in danger. And it had to stop.

He pressed Dean's contact and listened while it rang: once, twice...

"Hey," Dean answered, his voice soft as if he was whispering.

"Is she still unconscious?" Ryder asked, his pulse quickening with concern. Was that why Dean was whispering? He should have called an ambulance from the stairwell, but the Eagle Valley hospital was so far away that she would have been lying there on the cold landing for nearly an hour.

"She regained consciousness," Dean said. "Or so Dr. Ivan said. He had me step out, but when he let me back into the exam room, she was out again."

"Unconscious?"

"Sleeping," he said. "He's going to monitor her for a while and then determine if she needs to go to the hospital."

With people rushing from class to class, or drinking in their dorm rooms, falls down the stairwells were a common occurrence on campus. Most, fortunately, just got some bumps and bruises while a few unlucky ones needed to be sent to the hospital for broken bones or severe concussions.

"I respect Dr. Ivan." And he did, but the guy didn't deal with that many serious medical conditions anymore. "But it might be a good idea to get an ambulance out here to take her to the hospital now and have her thoroughly checked out. Taking a wait-and-see approach with her life is risky." And he should have followed his instinct to just drive her into town, but the campus clinic had been closer. And he truly did trust and respect Dr. Ivan. The man had "retired" from a busy hospital in Detroit to run the campus clinic, and there wasn't much the former emergency room doctor hadn't seen and didn't know how to treat. But this was Kristy…and Ryder wanted to make sure he didn't lose her like he had his mom and Mara.

Dean snorted. "You didn't wait and see. You took off the minute you dropped her in the clinic."

Ryder sucked in a breath, but their honesty with each other was why he and Dean were such good friends and for so long. "I came to the church," he explained.

Dean sucked in a breath that rattled the phone. "Really? I didn't know you're a religious man."

"I'm not."

"You're that worried about her?" he asked. "I'll make the call. I'll get an ambulance out here right away."

"Good," Ryder said, and that pressure on his chest eased a bit. But he knew it wouldn't lighten up much

more until she was gone. "And then you need to fire
her and send her away from St. Michel's."

Far away.

And even then Ryder didn't know if she would be
safe. Or if it was too late.

Had his bringing her back here put her in so much
danger that she wouldn't be able to escape it no matter where she was?

Kristy was conscious. But since she couldn't see
without her glasses and the light intensified her headache, she'd closed her eyes. And she'd kept them
closed when the provost had come into the room to
check on her.

She was still embarrassed over being caught eavesdropping outside his office. But embarrassment was
the least of her concerns right now. She had to be
careful about whom she trusted.

But then she'd heard Dean talking on his cell, and
he must have had his volume turned up high enough
that she could hear Ryder's deep voice, too. According to what she'd overheard, he was at the church.

She felt a surge of warmth over that; the church
was her favorite place to be. But clearly it wasn't
where he usually went or his friend wouldn't have
been so surprised. She waited until they ended their
call before she opened her eyes. Then she asked Dean,
"What are you going to do?"

He expelled a shaky sigh. "You are awake. I'm
going to call for an ambulance to bring you to the
hospital to make sure you're going to be okay."

"I'm okay," she said. But for her broken glasses. She had a spare set in her go-box back at her temporary apartment. How temporary was it going to be? "I don't need to go to the hospital." Maybe it was the painkillers Dr. Ivan had given her, but the pounding in her head wasn't as intense as it had been earlier.

Dean tilted his head and studied her face through narrowed, dark eyes. "Are you really? What happened after you ran out of my office? How upset were you about what you overheard?"

She tensed. "What? You think I threw myself down those stairs?" She sat up then, bristling with righteousness that he could have even thought that. Life was too precious to throw away for any reason.

"You just seemed really upset," he said.

Heat rushed to her face in embarrassment. The way she'd run away must have made the provost think she was some emotionally unstable person who couldn't handle confrontation and would do anything to avoid it. "I was," she admitted. "And I wanted to take some time before I talked to you."

"And Ryder?"

She wasn't sure she *wanted* to talk to him again. But she probably needed to. "I know he convinced you to hire me," she said. "And now he's trying to convince you to fire me. Are you going to?"

Dean uttered an uneasy sounding laugh. "I don't do everything Ryder wants," he said. "He's my friend. But I'm the boss."

"We both know you wouldn't have hired me without him pushing you to do it," she said.

He sighed. "Probably not. But you must not have heard everything he and I were saying in my office or you'd know that I'm very happy with this situation and would like to keep you on. But if you've changed your mind, if you want to leave…"

She should leave; she knew it was the smart thing to do. The safe thing…because she certainly wasn't safe here. "I don't think I fell down those steps," she said.

Dean looked at her with concern. "Don't you remember what happened?" he asked. He glanced toward the closed door, as if trying to conjure up the doctor again. "We really should take you to the hospital—"

"I didn't fall," she said again. "I was pushed."

His dark brows arched as his eyes widened with surprise. "What?"

"Someone pushed me."

A soft exhale slipped out of the man's mouth. "Ryder was right then. Your coming back here has put you in some kind of danger. He told me about what happened last night. That someone got into your place." He sighed. "I guess I can't blame you if you've decided to leave."

"*You* might not," she murmured.

"Ryder certainly won't blame you," he assured her. "That's why he wants me to let you go. He thinks bringing you here was a mistake."

She hadn't been talking about Ryder; she was well aware that he wanted her to leave. She was thinking about herself. She would definitely blame herself if she chickened out and ran off without finding out what was really going on. If she somehow could find Mara's murderer…

"But doesn't it prove what he's suspected all these years?" she wondered aloud.

"That you've been lying about Skip Holdren's alibi."

She gasped. "I haven't been lying," she insisted, her face flushing, but with anger, not embarrassment. "But someone must think I know something."

Dean shrugged. "Or this has nothing to do with Mara Lewis's murder, and someone just thinks you shouldn't be here, that you're not qualified for the job."

This time the heat in her face did come from embarrassment. "Who—who would think that?" she asked, even though she'd thought it herself so many times.

Dean offered her a weak smile. "I got a lot of calls and emails after I made the announcement about your class. We're primarily known as a literary arts college, so there's a lot of expectations for our professors to be…"

Better than her. That was how she'd felt all these years. Like she would never be as good and generous and spiritual as her missionary parents. Or even as full of promise as Mara had been.

That she just wasn't good.

"Do you want me to leave?" she asked.

He studied her face for a moment before he offered her another smile. This one was wider and seemed more genuine, but for his eyes…the smile didn't quite reach them, didn't quite warm them. "No, Kristy, I would very much like you to stay." And he reached out for her hand and took it in his. He rubbed his thumb across her skin. Maybe it was supposed to be a gesture of reassurance, but it made her uncomfortable instead.

Why did he want her to stay?

To teach? Or did he have some other reason for wanting her to stick around? A personal reason?

Once she would have been flattered had a man like Dean Stolz paid her any attention. She would have been flattered had any man paid her any attention. But after what had happened that night, how she'd thrown herself at Skip Holdren…she'd never wanted to catch a man's attention again.

Not that Skip had paid her any.

He'd loved Mara too much to take advantage of Kristy.

"How about you, Kristy?" Dean asked. "Do you want to stay?"

She sighed. "I don't want to," she honestly admitted. "But I will."

Instead of seeming pleased, Dean dropped her hand back onto the bed and stood up. "I better let Ryder know."

"Let me tell him," she said. The fact that she was staying wasn't all she wanted to share with him, though. She wanted to tell him about what had really happened on the stairs—that someone had pushed her. She swung her legs over the side of the bed and tried to stand, but as she did, her legs folded beneath her and she slid to the floor.

Dean dropped down next to her. "Are you okay?"

He tried to help her up, but she flinched as the pounding in her head intensified. "I just need to lie here a moment…" *And wait for the room to stop spinning.*

Dean pulled out his cell. "Ryder was right about you needing to go to the hospital," he said. "I'm going to call an ambulance right now."

She suspected the sudden movement had just made her a little dizzy and lightheaded, but she didn't fight him. She knew she needed all her faculties intact right now because she was in danger.

And she had to figure out why someone didn't want her back here…what they were afraid she might remember.

# Chapter Nine

The cold air chafed Ryder's skin as he urged Sable faster across the rolling hills. He'd been riding for over an hour, but he hadn't taken off across the campus until he'd seen that the ambulance had left…with Kristy.

She was getting checked out and treated, and they would probably keep her overnight for observation, so she would be safe the rest of the day and tonight. Tomorrow he would make sure she packed up all the stuff the state police had released, and he'd ensure that she left.

No prints but hers had been found on her boxes. As part of the application process to work at the college, everyone had to be fingerprinted while background checks were run on them. She had nothing on her record.

But that didn't mean she'd never done anything bad. She just hadn't been caught. He'd been so convinced she'd aided and abetted a killer, that she'd been an accessory after the fact. But now he wondered…

What was the real story about Kristy Kendall?

She'd lived with Mara, first in the dorms and then in their apartment, for nearly three years before Mara died. Mara must have known her well. And she'd considered the young woman her best friend. She'd always called her that when Ryder had talked to her on the phone or through text messages.

Text messages...

Anger squeezed his heart as he remembered those text messages Skip had sent his sister. Threats...

Far more serious threats than the vague one Kristy had found on her mirror. Had Skip written that to her? It didn't sound like his other ones. And why would he threaten the person who'd helped him evade justice?

Unless he hadn't evaded it at all.

Could Ryder have been wrong all these years?

Doubts and fears jumbled together in Ryder's mind; that was why he'd gone for the ride, to clear his head. But it continued to pound with confusion.

He doubted it hurt like Kristy's head must. Had she just slipped and fallen down those stairs? Or had something else happened?

He needed to talk to her. So he turned Sable toward home, hunkered down and rode her hard that last distance. Once he got to the stables, he took off her saddle and brushed her down before tucking her away in her stall with fresh water and food. He slid his hand over the velvety hair of her nose as he closed the door on her. "Good girl," he murmured. She'd been with him for years. During the rodeo circuit, back at the ranch and now here at a small private college in the upper peninsula of Michigan.

For some reason the horse seemed most content here…where Ryder was not. He was the restless and edgy one, like Sable had been on the circuit. He was the one who wouldn't relax until he got justice.

But was it going to forever elude him?

He'd thought Kristy was the key, and maybe she was. But he couldn't use her, couldn't risk her life, to flush out a killer. He'd rather the murderer came after him. After he stowed his saddle away in the tack room, he continued through to the small studio apartment behind it. The knob turned easily beneath his hand. Maybe he'd forgotten to lock the door before he'd gone for his ride. Or maybe…

Something clattered inside, like it had been knocked over or dropped. Ryder reached for his holster with the realization that maybe he'd gotten his wish and the killer had come for him.

He slowly opened the door and stepped inside with his gun drawn, his barrel pointed…at Kristy Kendall.

She gasped and raised her hands, dropping a plastic bowl back into a sink of sudsy water. "Don't shoot," she said.

He immediately lowered and reholstered his weapon. "What are you doing? Did you break into my place to do my dishes?"

A faint smile curved her lips. "No… I just got bored waiting for you to come back."

"Why are you here?" he asked.

"I needed to talk to you," she replied.

He shook his head. "No, why are you here and not in the hospital? Why didn't they keep you for observation?"

She shrugged. "I'm fine. The CT scan showed no cause for concern. And I just have some bumps and bruises." But she flinched when she moved, as if she was sore.

And here she was doing his dishes instead of resting.

"Sit down," he said, and he closed the distance between them to take her arm and guide her to a chair. But she flinched again when he touched her, and he jerked his hand away. "I'm sorry. You're really in pain, Kristy. You need to go back to the hospital."

She shook her head, and another grimace twisted her pretty features. She wasn't wearing her glasses. He hadn't seen them in the stairwell, but even if he'd found him, they'd probably been broken in her fall. "No, I'm not staying in the hospital. I'm going to stay here."

His pulse quickened. "What? Here?" He gestured at the size of the studio. A futon folded down into his bed, and when it was down, there was no room to walk between it and the trunk he used as a coffee table. The kitchen consisted of just a few cabinets and the sink on one of the walls, and a door on another wall opened to the small bathroom.

She must not have seen his gesture or realized what he thought she'd meant because she said, "I know you think I should leave St. Michel's, but that would be a mistake."

"Staying would be a mistake," he insisted. "Last night proved that, and what happened today?" He studied her face as he waited for her answer because when he'd been riding he'd started wondering…

Maybe she hadn't tripped and fallen.

And as the color receded from her face, he realized he was right. "Someone pushed you," he concluded.

She released a shaky sigh and nodded. "I felt a hand on my back, but maybe it was an accident…"

"The push was hard enough that you fell on your face," he said. "It wasn't like your foot just slipped on a step." He'd noticed that when he'd found her. But he hadn't found her. His friend had beaten him to her side. He glanced around, looking for the provost. "I thought Dean was with you."

"He was," she said. "He was with me at the hospital and then brought me back here and let me into your place to wait for you."

Dean was one of the few with a key. But then, like Ryder, he had a master key to everything that was campus owned. "He didn't stick around to wait with you."

"He had to return a bunch of calls," she said in her boss's defense. "He was really busy. And he had to either cover or cancel the class I was going to teach this afternoon." She grimaced again, as if she felt pain or guilt at not being able to teach.

Her class was the last thing she needed to be worried about right now. "I don't care what he had to do," Ryder said. "He shouldn't have left you here, unprotected."

"He thought you would be back soon because we saw you riding toward the stables when we drove onto the campus."

"And he wanted to get out of here before I came back," Ryder guessed.

"Maybe." She smiled. "He knows you're not going to be too happy with him." And Ryder could guess why even before she continued. "He's not going to fire me. He's not going to force me to leave. And neither are you."

"I'm not the one who messed with your stuff and wrote that note on the mirror, or pushed you down the stairs," Ryder said. "Kristy, I don't want you to get hurt again, maybe even worse than you've already been hurt..." Or dead. But he didn't even want to put that out there, to think of her dying. "That's why I want you to leave." The very last thing he wanted was anyone else getting hurt...but most especially not her.

She squinted and peered up at him as if she couldn't see him. "I don't understand you," she said. "You went through all this trouble to find me and get me here, and now you don't want me to stay."

"I don't want you to get hurt," he said.

"I thought you hated me." Her voice cracked with emotion.

"I don't hate you," he said. He'd learned long ago how that feeling poisoned from within, how even as a child it had made him feel sick. So when the carjacker had been arrested and jailed for his mother's murder, he'd let justice triumph over the hatred. Justice had not yet dealt with Mara's killer, though. "But

I couldn't understand why you would lie for him, why you would protect the killer of the woman who considered you her very best friend…" And his voice cracked with that emotion now.

Tears pooled in her eyes. "She *was* my best friend. And I would have never protected her killer. I want to find out who that is as badly as you do." She blinked furiously until the tears cleared away, and then she stood up straighter—as tall as her petite frame could go. "That's why I want to stay."

"But you said you don't know anything," he reminded her.

"And now you believe me?" she asked incredulously.

"I don't think you're lying," he admitted. "But I could be wrong." He could be wrong about a lot of things…maybe even Skip Holdren. "I can't imagine why anyone would hurt you unless you could hurt them somehow."

She shrugged. "I don't know how that would be, but I want to figure it out. I need your help to do that."

"What?" he asked, stunned that after all these years she was the one to suggest this.

"You brought me here," she said, "to get justice for Mara. I want that, too. Let's work together to find her killer."

Ryder should have been thrilled; this was all he wanted. All he'd thought about for the past ten years. But now that Kristy was willing to help him, his stomach muscles tightened with the sick feeling of dread and fear. He didn't want her in danger because he was beginning to care about her.

And he wanted that least of all.

Kristy had half expected Ryder to drive her off the campus instead of to the faculty apartment building. Then once he stopped his truck next to her car, she wouldn't have been surprised had he told her to get in it and drive away.

And never come back.

Instead he helped her out of the passenger side and up the stairs to the apartment he'd moved her to the night before. While he only guided her with his hand on her elbow, she remembered that sensation of being carried, and she knew his strong arms had been the ones wrapped around her. That sense of security, of safety, had been because of him.

But she didn't feel safe now. She was scared of the feelings, of the sudden rush of awareness she had for his warmth, for his strength, for even the smell of leather and horse and outdoors that clung to him. Overwhelmed with sensations and still not recovered from her fall, she felt too weak to walk up the stairs without his support, so she couldn't pull away from him physically. But emotionally she could remind herself that this attraction she felt for him was only going to lead to more pain for her, to more loss, because there was too much distrust and tragedy between them for them ever to have a future together. Because Mara had no future.

Ryder pulled physically away from her as he unlocked the door to her apartment. "The state police finished processing your first place and your stuff we left inside, but I thought you might prefer to stay in this unit instead of moving back to the other one," he said.

She shivered and nodded. "I do prefer this one." Where nobody had been inside, going through her things...leaving her cryptic messages. "Yes, thank you."

"Good, because I already had a couple security guards bring your things here after the state police techs were done."

She cleared her throat of the sudden rush of fear and asked, "Did the techs find anything?"

"Just your prints," he said. "We had them on file with your background check."

Remembering the process, she nodded. "The intruder must have worn gloves."

Ryder had had them on when he'd walked into his place a short while ago, but then he'd been out riding in the chilly spring air. She shivered at just the thought of how cold he must have been, with how fast his horse had been galloping across the grounds. Mara's one complaint about Eagle Valley had been the cold. She'd claimed her Texan blood preferred hot weather.

Was Ryder the same? He and his younger sister didn't look alike at all; he was dark-haired with those arresting blue eyes while Mara had been so blonde, like a ray of sunshine, with vivid green eyes that seemed to sparkle with life. Until that last day…

Kristy shivered now and remarked, "You didn't answer me."

"I just told you there were no prints," he said. "Are you having short-term memory issues? You really need to go back to the hospital—"

"No. You didn't answer me about Mara," she clarified. "About if you'll help me find her killer."

"Kristy, it's too dangerous," he said. "Surely you see that."

She smiled and pointed toward her face. "I can't see a whole lot right now." She found her go-box just inside the bedroom doorway and pulled out her backup pair of glasses with the black frames. But even with the lenses, her vision seemed a little blurred yet; he looked a little fuzzy. She closed her eyes for a moment as her head pounded. Whatever Dr. Ivan had given her at the clinic must have worn off, and while the ER doctor had given her a prescription, she hadn't taken any of those pills yet.

"You're hurt," he said. "And you need to get some rest for—"

"I have another class to teach," she interjected.

"That you already said Dean was working to cover," Ryder reminded her. "Trust me, the provost has got it handled. So don't worry about that class. Don't worry about anything but getting some rest, and then, when you're feeling stronger, we can pack up your car again and you can leave."

"I'm not leaving, Ryder, not until I know the truth."

He uttered a short chuckle. "That's what I said... three years ago when Dean hired me. I was just going to stay here until I got justice for Mara. At that time, it had already been seven years since her murder, so I should have known it wasn't going to be easy. But I was arrogant and foolish, and I thought it wouldn't take me long to find proof, to get evidence that the state police and the former head of campus security hadn't been able to find." He clenched his jaw so tightly that a muscle twitched along his cheek. Then he released it with a sigh. "Then another three years passed, and here we are...coming up on the tenth anniversary."

"That's why you put the pressure on Dean to hire me, to get me here," she surmised. "Because you thought I could help you, and you wanted charges brought against her killer before the anniversary."

"For ten years, I've wanted her killer put away," he said. "I wanted justice for Mara."

"Then let me help you," she urged. "With us working together, we'll figure it out."

"Or one of us will keep getting hurt," he said. "And I'm not willing to risk your life for justice."

"Not even for Mara?"

"Most especially not for Mara," he said. "She loved you. She would never forgive me if I let something happen to you."

"Then don't," she challenged him. "Keep me safe."

"The easiest, most effective way to do that is to get you off the campus and out of Eagle Valley."

Her head was pounding too hard to keep arguing with him, and she was so tired that she swayed slightly on her feet. "I can't do anything until I get some rest."

He nodded in agreement. "Of course. Let me know if you need anything. I'll stay out here while you sleep."

She furrowed her brow in confusion. "Why?"

"To keep you safe," he said. "You told me someone pushed you on those stairs, and last night…"

She sighed. "Last night I left the apartment door open. If I lock and dead bolt this one behind you, nobody will be able to get inside."

"But I know that with a concussion, you need to have someone checking on you, making sure you can wake up."

The problem wasn't going to be her waking up if he stayed in her place, but her getting to sleep at all. She shook her head. "That isn't necessary. But if you want to check on me, you can come back in an hour or so."

He hesitated for a long moment, and she reminded him, "You have the master key to let yourself back in to make sure that I'm all right."

He gave a slight nod of agreement. "Okay, but I'll be back in an hour."

"Maybe an hour and a half," she wheedled. She was really tired, but she didn't intend to sleep that entire time. Hopefully a half hour was all that she would need to regain some energy and dull the pain of her throbbing headache. But once she'd gotten some sleep, she wasn't leaving. She was even more determined to get to the truth. Whatever it was.

And wherever she had to go to get to the bottom of it.

# Chapter Ten

She was gone. He'd known it even before he used the master key to let himself inside her apartment. He knew it because her car was missing from the parking lot. Ryder checked inside her place to see if she'd packed up her stuff and taken off like he'd advised her to do. But just like the night before, she hadn't taken his advice.

Her boxes were still inside, along with a quilt on the couch where she must have taken a nap. He'd thought maybe she hadn't slept at all; maybe she'd just waited for him to leave before taking off.

But to where?

She hadn't shown up at the lecture hall where Dean was teaching her class. Ryder had gone there, hoping to talk some sense into his friend, but the provost had claimed to be too busy for conversation. And he'd probably been telling the truth.

Dean pretty much single-handedly ran St. Michel's. The president of the private college should have retired years ago; he had no interest in running the college and only stayed on because his social-ite wife enjoyed wining and dining the donors and alumni.

With how busy Dean was, Ryder should have been the one who'd taken Kristy to the hospital. Even if Dean wasn't busy, Ryder should have gone with her, and he shouldn't have left her now either. He was the one responsible for her coming back to St. Michel's, so he was responsible for keeping her safe…and for whatever happened to her if he didn't keep her safe. That would be his fault.

But he couldn't protect her if he couldn't find her.

Where had she gone?

She'd taken her car, so she'd probably left the campus. Or maybe with her concussion and bruises, she would have been too sore to walk and had decided to drive instead to wherever she'd wanted to go. So she could still be on campus. But…

The uneasy feeling in his gut told him she'd gone somewhere else, somewhere to get the answers she suddenly wanted about Mara's murder. He knew where he would go.

To the person Ryder had believed for the past ten years had killed his sister.

Kristy didn't believe Skip was responsible because she was the man's alibi. Ryder had thought she was lying before, but the more he got to know her, the more he wondered…

Who was wrong?

For this instance, desperate to find her, he would

check to see if she was at the Holdren estate. It adjoined the campus on the south side, between the college and the town of Eagle Creek. So it wasn't far.

He needed to be careful though because three years ago, when he'd first taken the job as head of campus security, he'd pressed too hard to get Skip to confess. And the man had accused him of harassment and taken out a restraining order against Ryder. Skip had also tried to use his leverage, with his family being a substantial benefactor of the college, to get Ryder fired.

But Skip hadn't left him threatening notes or messed with his stuff or pushed him down a flight of stairs.

So if he hadn't done those things to Ryder, who'd been determined to prove his guilt, why would he do those things to Kristy, who'd unwaveringly supported his claims of innocence all these years?

It didn't make sense.

Ryder rushed out of her apartment and jumped in his vehicle. He couldn't risk driving his easily recognizable truck over there. So he stopped at the stables and saddled up Sable again. On horseback, it would be harder to spot him—especially as the sun was starting to slip away, leaving shadows among the trees and hills.

Nudging his knee slightly against Sable's side, he urged her to go faster, to close the distance between them and the Holdren estate. It wasn't far, and soon he was pulling up to the fence that separated it from the college. He skirted around to the street side until he could see the driveway.

Her car was parked there near the front door. His pulse quickened, pounding fast and hard with panic. Ryder had believed this man was a killer for so long—his every instinct screaming that Skip was Mara's murderer—that his first instinct now was to climb that fence and get to Kristy, to make sure Skip didn't hurt her like he had Mara.

But Ryder finally had to acknowledge that he could have been wrong all these years—if Kristy was right. And even if he was right and she was wrong, it was still unlikely that Skip would try to hurt Kristy in his home with his wife and kids and, from the other cars in the driveway, additional guests around to witness his crime.

They would also be around to witness Ryder violating that restraining order if he climbed over the fence. And then he'd lose his job for certain because Dean had already warned him that he wouldn't back him up if he broke the law. But he didn't want another woman getting hurt with him doing nothing to protect her. And if Skip hurt Kristy, breaking the law would be the least of Ryder's concerns.

*This is a mistake.*

Kristy knew it the minute she left her place without waiting for Ryder to come back. But he'd made it clear he didn't want her help investigating his sister's murder. He just wanted her to leave.

And she wasn't leaving Eagle Valley until she

knew who had killed Mara. And who had come after her now.

Why?

Did she already know who had killed her friend, but for some reason she'd blocked it from her mind? Her memory was so hazy from that party Skip had thrown. He hadn't been living at home, but in one of the fraternity houses on campus.

The last thing Kristy had wanted to do was attend a frat party, but Mara had insisted she come along and let her hair down for once. And the music, the dancing, the laughing…she had started out enjoying it. Skip had always been fun, just like Mara. He'd often teased Kristy like a big brother would a little sister over silly stuff—over all the pop culture references she didn't know, all the movies she'd never seen…since she'd spent so much time outside the US.

She'd even been to his house once when Mara had insisted she tag along to meet his parents, almost as if she hadn't believed Skip that they would be there. So Kristy had been at the Holdren estate before. She'd known which button to push on the intercom at the big gate in the wrought iron fence that surrounded the property, but before she'd been able to reach for it, the gates had creaked open. And a man on a motorcycle had stopped beside her car.

He wore no helmet, but his long dark hair was matted down like he had been wearing one. He looked vaguely familiar to her, but he certainly wasn't Skip. Skip had been nicknamed The Golden Boy for more than his family money; he'd been as blond as Mara.

This man tapped on her window, which she quickly rolled down. "Who are you?" he asked.

"I'm an old friend of—"

Before she could answer, he tapped that intercom button for her. "Mrs. Holdren, I'm letting someone in to see you. Says she's an old friend..."

"Of Skip's," Kristy said, raising her voice so that the person on the other end of the intercom could hear her, too. "I'm an old friend of Skip's from St. Michel's." That was all they'd ever been, despite that night, despite what other people had thought.

"Let her through," Mrs. Holdren replied. "See you tomorrow, Joey."

"Sure thing..." he said. Then he stood there, over his idling motorcycle, until Kristy drove through the gates. And in her rearview mirror, she saw him staring after her car for a moment before he turned around, settled onto his seat and peeled off down the street.

When she shut off her engine, she could still hear his, howling as he drove away. She drew in a shaky breath and pushed open the driver's door, then stepped out on the brick paver driveway. A groan slipped out as her bruised body protested the movement. She'd tried to rest, but deep sleep had eluded her. Her mind had been too full, too jumbled, with thoughts of Mara.

And Ryder...

She'd kept imagining him carrying her, staring down at her with those blue eyes of his. Protecting her...

Was that really why he wanted her to leave now? To keep her safe?

She didn't deserve his concern. Not if there was something she could have done that night to save his sister.

She had to know. So she walked to the front door that a woman held open for her. She wasn't old enough to be Skip's mother, who Kristy had assumed had answered the buzz of the intercom. This woman was Kristy's age, Mara's age…and so very familiar with her bright blond hair and cold blue eyes.

"I heard you were back in Eagle Valley, but I never thought you'd have the guts to show up here," Amy Towers bitterly remarked. Then she opened the door wider and called out to someone else. "Gretchen, look, it really is her. And she hasn't changed a bit."

From the snarl in Amy's voice, it was clear she didn't consider that a compliment, and Kristy knew not to take it as one. Amy Towers and Gretchen Manchester had been popular girls on campus—sorority sisters as well as equestrian team members of Mara's. They'd wanted Mara to pledge their sorority, but she'd refused unless they would have allowed Kristy to pledge as well. And they'd refused.

They'd claimed it was because she wasn't part of the equestrian team. But Kristy knew they found her lacking in more than horsemanship. And clearly they still did.

Gretchen stepped around the door and stared down her nose at Kristy. "Wow…you're not kidding."

Amy and Gretchen had often teased her like Skip had, but from them, it had seemed mean-spirited. And Mara had always called them out on it and made them stop. She'd protected Kristy. But when she'd needed Kristy's protection...

Kristy would never forgive herself for not being there for her.

"What are you doing here?" Amy asked.

"I could ask you the same thing," Kristy pointed out, but maybe it was good that they were here. They could help her fill in some of the missing pieces from that night since they'd been at the party, too.

"This is her house," Gretchen said, the brunette snarling at her with the same disdain Amy had showed her. "And I'm here because I'm really a friend. Not the kind of friend you proved to be."

She couldn't argue with them, and she really didn't want to.

But before she could say or ask them anything, Amy remarked, "What? You came here looking to throw yourself at Skip again the minute you got back in town and didn't expect to find me here? Skip and I are married, Kristy. We've been married for eight years, and we have two children. Don't you read the alumni newsletter?"

"I'm not on the mailing list," she replied. Once she'd graduated, she'd wanted to forget about St. Michel's college. She hadn't wanted to forget Mara, though. And finally now she had enough courage to try to honor her as she already should have.

"You should sign up," Gretchen said. "It's a great way to learn what's going on with our former classmates, like one of them crawling back to campus for a job she's not even qualified to do."

Amy snorted. "Guess it helps to have pull with the provost."

Gretchen giggled then. "A lot of us had pull with the provost."

Amy smiled. "Especially Mara…"

"I came here to talk about Mara," she admitted. "To ask about her—"

"You were supposed to be her best friend," Gretchen said. "You were supposed to be the closest to her."

"But then you betrayed her—" Amy finished when the brunette trailed off "—throwing yourself at her boyfriend like you did."

Kristy could have asked how Amy had wound up married to him, but that apparently hadn't happened until a couple of years after Mara's death. And she should have been happy for them, that they'd managed to move on.

She hadn't.

And neither had Ryder.

"I don't remember much of that night," Kristy admitted. "That's why I'm here. I'm hoping to find some answers."

Amy snorted. "Like that's all you want from Skip."

"What?" a male voice asked.

Kristy jumped and whirled around to find a man had walked up behind her. She hadn't heard him approach. She also hadn't heard the sports car drive up, but there was now a red vehicle parked next to her clunker and the couple of other vehicles that had already been there. Skip stood right behind her.

His sudden appearance had a chill slithering down

her spine. Had she let Ryder's suspicions about Skip being a killer get to her? Or was she just on edge after what had happened the past couple of days since she'd been back on campus?

Skip's appearance itself was much the same as it had been ten years ago. His blond hair was still thick and expertly styled, and his skin was still tan despite it barely being spring. Maybe he and Amy had just returned from a vacation someplace warmer and sunnier than northern Michigan.

His brown eyes widened in surprise. "Kristy Kendall. I wondered whose car that was."

"Hi Skip," she said. "I know I should have called first..." But she'd figured she would have lost her nerve over the phone, and it was better for her to talk to him in person.

"Nonsense," he said. "My home is always open to an old friend." He glanced at his wife who stood blocking the doorway. "Why haven't you welcomed Kristy inside?"

She stepped back then, almost stumbling in her haste. "I didn't think you'd want to see her."

"Why wouldn't I?" he asked his wife. Then he pressed his hand lightly against Kristy's back to guide her over the threshold into his home.

She tensed at his touch, as the hand on her back reminded her of the other hand she'd felt—the one that had propelled her down the stairs of the administration building. Not that she believed he'd done that. She would have seen him. But after she'd fallen, she hadn't seen anyone.

"Please, come inside," he urged. He must have sensed her hesitation. "Despite how catty Amy and Gretchen are acting, you're very welcome here."

She drew in a breath and stepped inside then. As she did, Gretchen and Amy walked away, as if they had no more interest in her. That was what had happened every time Mara had stopped them from picking on her; they'd lost interest.

"Come into my den," Skip said as he stepped through a set of double doors into a paneled room. "I was happy to see in the alumni newsletter that you were coming back. I intended to let you settle into your new role and then see how you've been."

Once she joined him inside, he closed those doors, and that sudden chill rushed over her again. While she knew she was letting Ryder's suspicions—no, his certainty—that Skip was a killer get to her, she had to consider that he could be right. And if he was, then she was now alone with a killer.

She wasn't actually alone with him, though. She could hear other voices outside those double doors. Children chattering, and Amy and Gretchen answering them. "Until now, I didn't know you and Amy got married," she said. "Congratulations."

He made a slight grimace but then chuckled. "We're happy…most of the time. How about you, Kristy? I've worried about you often over the years. You took Mara's death so hard. It was like you were blaming yourself…"

She sighed and admitted, "I do."

"You weren't even there," he said.

"And maybe that's why she died."

"Maybe it's why you both didn't die," he said. "And you're being too hard on yourself about what happened. You had never had a drink, so it hit you hard. You got sick and passed out."

In his bed...

That was where she'd woken up the next day, wearing his clothes. He'd been sleeping on the floor, though, next to a bucket. He'd taken care of her.

Like she should have taken care of Mara.

"I don't remember so much of that night..." The music. The dancing. The laughing. And that drink...

"Yeah, that's what happens when you get blackout drunk," he said. "And you're not the only one who's ever done that. Stop beating yourself up about it." He studied her face for a long moment. "Or is someone else beating you up about it? Ryder Lewis?"

Heat rushed to her face at the thought of him, but Skip must have mistaken her blush for acknowledgement.

"I knew it," he said. "No offense, but when you got hired, I figured he was behind it. That he'd coerced his old friend into making the job offer."

She flinched, but she couldn't deny that was what had happened.

Skip shook his head. "He just can't let it go."

"Nobody's been charged with Mara's murder," she said. "He just wants justice for his sister."

Skip snorted. "Stepsister. Didn't you wonder why they look nothing alike? They're not even related. And there's something weird about his obsession with her. I told the state police they should have checked to see where he was when she was killed."

"I'm sure he had nothing to do with that," she said. "And Mara always called him her brother." And she'd loved him so very much. While Kristy hadn't met him until the memorial, she'd overheard Mara talking to him so many times and had been included on the pictures Mara had sent him, much to her chagrin.

He shrugged again. "Who knows what really happened. A lot of people were obsessed with Mara."

"Who?" she asked. She'd been aware back then that everyone who'd met the vivacious blonde had been drawn to her, but had someone been unnaturally attached to her?

Skip gestured her toward a chair while he sat on the edge of his desk. Then he told her what she'd come there to ask him: everything he remembered from back then. And when he was done, she was reeling, trying to process all she'd learned.

"Want to stay for dinner?" he asked her.

Thinking of seeing Amy and Gretchen again had her stomach churning. She shook her head and rushed toward the front door, then pulled it open to step out into the night. Despite the gas lanterns on the old brick house casting only faint light, Kristy felt exposed, like someone was watching her.

She rushed toward her car, jumped inside and prayed that it would start, that she could escape. But she wasn't sure if she was running from the house or from everything she'd learned. Ryder wasn't really Mara's brother?

What else had he kept from her? Did he know about all the other possible suspects? Was Skip right? Was Ryder focused on proving him guilty in order to protect someone else?

Thankfully the motor turned over, and she was able to drive through the gates Skip, or probably Amy, had opened for her. The road was even darker than the driveway. So dark she wasn't sure what happened.

One minute she was driving toward the college...

The next she heard a loud noise, a bang, and then the steering wheel jerked in her hands, propelling her toward the ditch. She tried to fight it, tried to get back onto the pavement, but it was as if she'd lost all control of the vehicle. Another bang rang out, the wheel jerked again and the car swerved straight into the ditch. The last thing Kristy saw before the air bag exploded in her face was the dark silhouette of a man on a horse.

# Chapter Eleven

*Gunshots!*

The sudden blast of the first shot had Sable rearing up, nearly toppling Ryder out of the saddle. He clasped the horse's sides with his legs, using his body to hang on while he clutched the reins in one hand. His other hand reached for his weapon. But before he could even draw it, another blast rang out.

And tires squealed, then flapped against the pavement as the vehicle lost control and spun into the ditch.

*Kristy!*

His first instinct had been that the shots had been meant for him, but now it was apparent where they'd been fired: into Kristy's car.

He fought with Sable, and urged her toward the running vehicle, even as she tried to shy back. Once she was close, he jumped down from her back but held tightly to her reins yet. He couldn't let her slip away, not when he might need her to escape. And to help Kristy escape.

If she was unharmed.

*Please, God, let her be all right.*

He shouldn't have worried about violating that stupid personal protection order Skip had taken out against him. He should have only been worried about her.

Even more than Mara.

Mara was gone. Nobody could hurt her anymore.

But Kristy was here.

And she was already wounded.

*Please, God, let her be okay.*

He hurried toward the driver's side of the vehicle, but all he could see through the window was the air bag. Then small hands slapped at it—pushing it aside—and Kristy's head appeared. She was conscious. It wasn't like when he'd found her on the stairs.

But then another shot rang out, startling Sable again so that she nearly tugged away from his grasp on her reins. Instead of drawing his gun with his free hand, Ryder reached for the door handle, trying to open it, but the handle came off in his fingers.

Kristy slammed her body against it on the inside, struggling to push it open, but the door caught against the hard ground of the ditch which held it shut. He pointed at the window, indicating she needed to lower it. Then he peered around in the dark, trying to determine from where the shots were coming.

The Holdren estate.

He was sure of it. Kristy had only made it a short

distance from the wrought iron gates before the first shot had rung out and then the second.

And now another one.

Sable cried in fear and reared up again, but he held her still as he drew his weapon and fired back in that direction as he kept his body in front of Kristy and hoped he and the vehicle shielded her as she crawled through the window she'd lowered. Once she was out, he holstered his gun and climbed into the saddle. Then he reached down and lifted her up in front of him. Using his knees against Sable's sides, he urged the horse to run toward the campus and hopefully to safety.

And as they rode away, he braced himself for the next bullet... The one that would probably hit his back if it was fired now. Because he'd made sure to put himself between Kristy and danger.

He didn't want to lose another woman he was coming to care about...despite all his reasons not to fall for her.

Kristy's head had already been pounding from the concussion; now it pounded with the echo of the gunshots and the horse's hooves against the ground as it ran toward the stable. She clutched at its mane and the saddle horn, trying to hang on even as Ryder's strong arms wrapped around her and cradled her in front of him.

Protecting her.

She braced herself for the ride and for more shots. But they must have traveled far enough out of range of gunfire. She heard nothing but the sound of the horse's hooves and, in the distance, the faint sound of an engine.

A car. Or that motorcycle she'd seen earlier?

"Ryder?" she whispered, her voice hoarse—probably from screaming when she'd first gone in the ditch and the air bag had exploded in her face.

He slowed the horse. And she worried that he was stopping for her or, worse yet, because he was hurt. But then she noticed the lights of the stable ahead. "We're here," he said as he rode the horse through the open doors of the barn as if he hadn't wanted to dismount outside because he was worried they might still be in danger.

Were they?

Would the shooter follow them onto campus?

"Are you all right?" she asked.

He slid off the horse behind her and then reached up, wrapped his hands around her waist and lifted her down onto the barn floor. "Are *you* all right?" he asked, his voice gruff with concern.

She nodded.

"You didn't get hurt?" he asked, as if he didn't believe her.

"No. I don't know what happened..."

"The bullets must have hit your car," he said, "because you veered off the road into the ditch."

"I lost control," she admitted.

"I think they shot out the tires," he said.

She nodded again. "That's what it felt like—a tire blowout..." And maybe that was what someone would have believed if she'd been killed. And if Ryder hadn't been there, she might have been. She could have died in the crash, or maybe the shooter would have approached her vehicle—if Ryder hadn't beaten them to her—and made certain she hadn't survived. "Thank you for getting me out of there."

"You really didn't get hurt?" he asked again, and he reached up to cup her cheek in his palm.

Her skin tingled where he touched her. "No, the air bag saved me from hitting my head, but it knocked off my glasses." She'd found them on the console, and fortunately they hadn't been broken. She'd managed to put them back on before crawling out the window and into Ryder's arms.

"The frames might be a little bent," he said, and he moved his hand from her cheek to touch the rim above her nose. "But the lenses aren't even scratched."

"Too bad there hadn't been an air bag on those stairs earlier today," she said, ruing the loss of her favorite pair of glasses as well as gaining the bumps and bruises and concussion she had.

He chuckled uneasily, then pulled his hand from her face and reached for his cell phone. "I'm going to call the police," he said. "You need to go into my place and lock all the doors. And don't open them to anyone but me when I get back from the crash site."

She grabbed his arm. "You can't go back out there. The shooter could still be out there..." Waiting for Ryder to return. "I don't think the shots that were fired after I went in the ditch were intended for me."

His lips parted as if he'd gasped, and he nodded,

knocking the brim of his black hat lower over his eyes. Then he started speaking about the location, possible caliber and the make and model of her vehicle, and she realized he was talking to a police dispatcher. He gave his name and position at St. Michel's and then her name as well. "Yes," he replied. "I'll make sure she stays safe until a trooper can come out to take our statements. We'll be on St. Michel's campus, in the small apartment attached to the stables."

After ending the call, he led his horse to a stall and removed its saddle. Kristy stood frozen in the middle of the barn, remembering the times Mara had convinced her to tag along here. Mara had loved the stables. "The last time I was on a horse was with your sister…" she murmured. Then she remembered what Skip had told her. "Mara was your sister, right?"

He turned toward her then, his blue eyes narrowed as he studied her face. "Are you sure you're not having side effects from that concussion? Confusion?"

"No, Skip told me—"

"You must have lost your mind to go there by yourself," he said. "To put yourself in that kind of danger."

"He didn't hurt me," she said. "I wasn't in danger until I left. Maybe I should have accepted his invitation to stay for dinner." But she shuddered as she considered how well Amy and Gretchen would have treated their unwelcome guest. She almost wouldn't put it past one of them to have fired those shots at her, to have caused her to drive into the ditch. While they were still the mean girls they'd been ten years ago, she doubted that either of them was a killer, though.

Ryder shook his head. "You can't trust Skip Holdren. You can't trust anything he told you."

"He told me that you and Mara weren't related," she said.

"She was my sister."

"Stepsister?"

He sighed. "Half sister. Her mom is my stepmother, my dad's second wife."

That probably explained why they didn't look much alike, although she'd known twins who hadn't resembled each other at all. "I didn't realize. Mara only ever called you her brother."

"I am. I was…" After taking care of the horse, he backed out of the stall, with the saddle hoisted on one of his broad shoulders, and closed the door, but he didn't look at her.

And she knew there was more. "What is it?" she asked. "What aren't you telling me?" What had Mara never told her about him? She'd thought she and her best friend had been so close that they'd known everything about each other. But Skip had told her things she hadn't known and reminded her of things she'd forgotten.

Ryder glanced around, as if worried that someone else might be in the barn. Then he took her arm and led her through the tack room, where he deposited the saddle, before escorting her back into his small studio apartment. "I can't imagine why Skip brought up any of that…except that he probably wanted to deflect from his own guilt."

"He doesn't need to," she said. "He has an alibi."

Ryder nodded. "Yes. And I do, too. I was over a thousand miles away at a rodeo that was televised, so if you have any doubts about me, you can find old footage of it to prove my innocence. But I hope you know I would have never hurt Mara. She was my baby sister. She made me believe in the good in the world again."

Confusion and her headache made her furrow her brow and grimace. "You can't be that much older than she was."

"Eight years," he said.

"How did you lose your belief that there is good in the world at eight years old?" she asked, thinking of the children she'd met through her parents' missionary work—of their wide-eyed wonder despite the atrocities so many of them had seen and endured.

"I was actually six…when my mother was murdered in front of me at a stoplight for the SUV my dad had just bought her."

Pain jabbed her heart with the knowledge of the atrocity he'd witnessed and endured. "Oh, no. Were you hurt?"

"He pulled her body out of the driver's seat of the SUV first and then he pulled me out of the back seat, and he put the gun to my head…" A shaky breath slipped out of his lips. "But he didn't pull the trigger."

She found herself reaching out to him and slid her arms around his lean waist to offer him the warmth and support of a hug. Or maybe to find warmth and support herself as sympathy for him overwhelmed her. "I'm so sorry, Ryder…"

"That he didn't shoot me?" He chuckled, but it sounded rusty and forced.

She gently squeezed him. "I'm so sorry you went through such a horrible experience at such a young age."

"I felt so helpless that I couldn't save her..." His deep voice cracked with emotion as it trailed off.

"You were only six years old," she said. "That the carjacker didn't kill you...was God's intervention."

"Why me?" he asked, and he stepped back from her to peer down into her face as if he thought she had the answers. His eyes were damp with unshed tears. "Why not intervene for her? Why not for Mara?"

Tears stung Kristy's eyes, too, and she shook her head. "I don't know...maybe so you could save someone else...as a Marine and in the rodeo and here at the college...like you saved me tonight. But I know that's not the same, and it's little comfort after losing women you loved like your mom and your sister."

Mara had been more than just a sibling to him; Skip had been right about that. But she hadn't been an obsession; she'd been his salvation. His belief that there was good in the world again. And she had been so good.

"Thank you for saving me tonight," she said. "I don't even know how you happened to be there. That must have been God's intervention as well."

His long, lean body shuddered as if he was reliving the moment her car had gone in the ditch. "That was just me figuring out where you must have gone after I showed up at your place and saw that you'd skipped out on me. I knew you wanted to investigate Mara's murder, and who would know more about it than the man who committed it?"

She shook her head. "Skip didn't do it, Ryder."

"Yeah, right, that's why he's trying to make you think I did it." He snorted in derision.

"He mentioned you, yes," she said. "But he brought up other possible suspects, too. Reminded me of things I forgot."

He narrowed his eyes in skepticism but asked, "Like what?"

"Like how, on the day before she died, Mara caught someone right here at the stables stealing ketamine from the veterinarian's truck. It was a fellow student. She knew who it was and was going to report him, but she never got the chance."

Ryder shook his head. "So there's conveniently no one to corroborate this story."

"There's me," she said. "I remembered it when Skip was talking about it. I remember Mara being so upset and not knowing who to tell about it."

"The head of security," Ryder said. "She would have told the head of security if it had actually happened."

"The person she caught stealing the drugs was the son of the head of security…" And she trailed off as she remembered why the guy on the motorcycle had looked so familiar. She'd seen him around here before on campus, but she couldn't remember exactly where. At the stables? But why would he have been working at Skip's family estate?

"Are you sure you really remember this happening? Or did Skip plant that memory in your head?" he asked. "You never mentioned it before."

"It's been so hard for me to think back to that time," she said. "That's one of the reasons why I never returned the messages you left for me with the relatives you called when you were trying to track me down. The main reason is that I can't tell you what you want to hear—that I wasn't with Skip the night Mara was killed."

He grimaced as if the thought of her being with Skip sickened him. It would have sickened her, too, if something had happened. But she knew it hadn't.

"It wasn't like that," she said. "I was drunk, and I made a fool of myself."

"And Skip took advantage."

"He didn't," she assured him. "Your predecessor thought that, too, and made me have a medical examination. Nothing happened with Skip. He was a perfect gentleman."

He snorted in derision again. "Yeah, *that* you remember but nothing else...until you talked to Skip tonight."

"Usually when I think back to that time, I just remember that morning I found her." She shuddered now as she relived that horror. "That's why I didn't want to think about it or talk about it and relive that nightmare."

He slid his arms around her in a comforting hug. "I'm sorry. I know what that's like...to be haunted by something that's happened..."

"You do." And he'd only been six years old when that nightmare had started for him. "I'm sorry you lost your mom to a senseless act of violence, and that you witnessed it. That must have been so terrifying and traumatizing. Did they ever catch the carjacker?" She leaned back in his arms to peer up into his face.

He nodded. "Yes, but it took nearly a year. I identified him in a lineup and testified against him in court."

She gasped. "But you were so young…"

"It made me feel better," he said. "Made me feel less helpless, less useless."

"That's why I went to Skip's tonight," she said. "I wanted to feel less helpless. Less useless."

"So what else did Skip tell you?" he asked, but he sounded skeptical yet.

"He told me how much he loved Mara," Kristy recalled. And she'd believed it from the tears in his eyes and the break in his voice. He really had loved her.

"You can't call the way he treated her love." Ryder pulled away from her and fisted his hands at his sides. "You want to see the texts and letters he sent her? Talk about obsession. Those are why I'm convinced he killed her, Kristy. He knew he couldn't have her, and he didn't want anyone else to."

She nodded. "There was that," she said. "He admitted to sending some stupid stuff, to being a spoiled only child who had always got what he'd wanted until Mara…"

Ryder sucked in a breath. "You got him to confess?"

She sighed. "To being a spoiled rich kid but not to

murder. He knew Mara didn't return his feelings for her. While he loved her, she was in love with someone else."

"Who?"

"Your best friend. *Dean Stolz.*"

He chuckled and shook his head. "Yeah, right..."

"Ryder..."

He narrowed his eyes and studied her face. "What are you saying? Skip made you remember something about Dean, too?"

She shook her head. "No. *I* remember. Dean is a big part of the reason Mara wanted to come to St. Michel's."

Ryder smiled. "I wanted her to come here because of Dean, so he could keep an eye on her and keep her safe." His smile slipped away.

Dean had failed. Just like she had.

"She really was crazy about him," Kristy said. "She took every class he taught. And while a lot of other people couldn't get into his courses, she always managed."

"Like I said, I asked him to keep an eye on her, to watch over her," Ryder murmured. But clearly he realized his friend had failed him and Mara.

"There were rumors, back then, about him and students," Kristy admitted.

Ryder shook his head. "He was married."

"Yeah, and if anyone could prove those rumors were true, his marriage and his career would have been over." And instead, his career had flourished; he'd become the provost.

Ryder shook his head again. "Then why offer me a job? Why bring me here when he knows I'm determined to find Mara's killer?"

She shrugged. "Maybe he figured you were so convinced that it's Skip that you wouldn't look at anyone else, especially someone you know and trust."

The color drained from Ryder's face.

"I'm sorry," she said. "I don't want you to doubt your friend." Or worse yet: to doubt himself.

She knew how that felt. How it was to lose faith, especially in yourself.

## Chapter Twelve

Ryder barely listened as Kristy gave her report to the state trooper. She hadn't seen the shooter either, so neither of them had been able to give a description or anything else to go on. He'd wanted to accuse Skip, but Ryder had no proof that the former frat boy had taken those shots at them.

Ryder had no actual evidence that the man had murdered Mara.

Was that because Skip was innocent?

And someone else, someone Ryder had trusted, was guilty?

He had to talk to Dean. Ryder barely waited until the door closed behind the trooper before he started out after him. But as she had earlier, Kristy grabbed his arm, her slim fingers clutching at the sleeve of his jacket.

"Where are you going?"

"To talk to someone," he said.

"Dean or Skip?"

"Dean." He sighed. "Skip has a personal protection order sworn out against me. That's why I didn't jump over the gate when I saw your car parked on his estate earlier today. But I probably should have ignored it and risked him calling the cops on me."

"Why?" she asked. "I wasn't in danger on the estate. And we have no proof that he had anything to do with the shots fired at me or with Mara's murder."

He uttered a deep groan and pushed a hand through his hair, knocking his hat from his head onto the hardwood floor.

Kristy crouched to pick it up, but when she stood, she swayed slightly on her feet. And instead of taking the hat from her, Ryder closed his arms around her to steady her.

"Are you all right?" he asked, his heart pounding with concern for her while his head pounded with recrimination for himself. "After you got out of your crashed car, I should have taken you back to the hospital. I really should have done that right when you showed up this afternoon. With the concussion you have, it's too dangerous for you to have left."

"I'm glad I did," she said. "I feel like I learned a lot today."

He blew out a ragged breath that stirred the silky brown hair that had pulled free of her bun. "You learned more in one day than I learned in nearly ten years," he admitted. "So much for my criminal justice degree…" And his instincts. After reading those texts and letters and suspecting that Skip's alibi was contrived, Ryder had been so certain Mara's boyfriend had killed her that Ryder hadn't considered anyone else.

"I'm sorry," she murmured.

"You don't owe me an apology," he said. "In fact I owe you one." He touched her chin, tipping her face up to his. "It's long overdue. I'm sorry I was so rude to you at Mara's memorial. I'm sorry I've tried to track you down all these years."

"And coerced Dean into hiring me as adjunct professor?" she asked. "Are you sorry about that?"

He sighed. "I'm sorry I put you in danger," he said. "If I had any idea… But I was just so blindly focused on getting justice for Mara that I didn't realize someone might try to hurt you. You need to leave St. Michel's. You need to leave Eagle Valley."

"I'm not going anywhere until we find out who killed Mara," she said.

"No," he said. "I'm not going to risk you getting killed while we try to find her killer. Mara wouldn't have wanted that."

Tears glistened in Kristy's dark eyes, and she stepped back, pulling away from his touch as if she couldn't bear it. And she just shook her head.

His hand dropped back to his side, but he was tempted to reach for her again. He had the sudden urge to hold her, to kiss her—which was crazy. The last thing he wanted was to get involved with Kristy Kendall. He avoided relationships because he didn't want to risk losing anyone the way he'd lost his mom and Mara. And with someone already trying to kill Kristy, she was at more risk than anyone else he knew.

Except him.

He wasn't just at risk of getting shot, like earlier tonight; he was in danger of falling for her.

"For Mara's sake, please quit this job and leave," he urged her. "She wouldn't want anything to happen to you."

She blinked furiously, but still a tear fought free of her lashes and rolled down her cheek and beneath her glasses. "She's why I need to stay. Why I need to do this. I owe her an apology and so much more for what happened," she said. "I need to make it up to her."

Clearly he wasn't the only one who felt as if he'd failed Mara. "Tell me, Kristy. Tell me everything you remember about that night and that morning."

The color drained from her face, and more tears streaked down her cheeks, dripping from her chin. And he knew what he was asking was too much, just like bringing her to St. Michel's had been too much, too dangerous for her life and for her peace of mind.

Kristy closed her eyes, but she couldn't hold back the tears. Maybe she was just too tired to fight them, or maybe they were just so long overdue that she couldn't suppress them any longer.

Strong arms closed around her and held her as she shook with sobs. "Shhh…" he murmured. "I'm sorry. I'm so sorry I asked. Just forget it. I'll get you back to your apartment. You need to rest."

She couldn't argue with that. She should have slept longer today, especially with the way her head was pounding now. But she also had no regrets about finding out all that she had, about finally pursuing justice for Mara.

Her only regret was that she hadn't done it ten years ago. She'd trusted other people to find Mara's killer. Maybe, like Ryder, she'd trusted the wrong people.

He started guiding her, with his strong arms wrapped loosely around her, across the room, but she dug in her heels. Then she opened her eyes and pulled back from him. She didn't deserve his comfort. Or the apology he'd offered her earlier.

He deserved more from her—*her* apology and everything she could remember from that horrible time. But she was reluctant to tell him the truth, reluctant to have him look at her again like he had at the memorial, with such disgust and disdain.

She shouldn't have cared what he thought; he was Mara's brother but he was nothing to her. And he would never be.

Clearly he'd closed himself off from relationships after losing his mom and Mara. The one person who was still close to him, Dean, might have betrayed that friendship. And if that was the case, she doubted he would ever let anyone else into his trust or into his heart.

Not that she wanted to get into his heart. She'd done nothing yet to deserve anyone's love, especially not his.

"I don't want to talk about that night," Kristy admitted.

"I'm sorry I asked. You don't need to relive that."

"I don't want to talk about it," she repeated. "But I

need to... I need to relive that night." It was the right thing to do, and she'd put off doing the right thing for far too long.

"Kristy—"

"This is what you wanted me to do," she reminded him. "It's why you've tried to track me down all these years. It's why you convinced Dean to offer me the adjunct professor job."

He sighed. "That was a mistake. Ever since you've been back, you've been in danger, been threatened and nearly killed. I can't risk your life anymore."

"You're not," she said. "I'm choosing to stay for my sake and for Mara's. I need to do this as much for me as for her." She was never going to forgive herself until she'd done everything she could to help bring Mara's killer to justice.

"You've already done more than I have," he said. "You got Skip to talk to you."

She sighed. "But now I'm not sure how much of it was true. He was wrong about you and Mara."

Ryder grimaced. "I guess I was obsessed with keeping her safe, and that overprotectiveness might have made our relationship seem unhealthy."

"After what happened to your mom, your overprotectiveness was certainly understandable," she said. And in the end he'd been right to worry about Mara; she had been in danger.

Mortal danger.

"And it would be understandable for you to want to put all this behind you, Kristy," he said.

"I can't," she said. "I tried. All these years I've tried,

but I can't let Mara go any more than you've been able to. We both need to find out the truth about what happened to her, so please, let me tell you what I remember, and let's work together to get her justice."

He opened his mouth as if he was going to argue with her again.

But she reached up and pressed her finger over his lips. "Please, let me do this."

He closed his mouth and nodded.

Her finger tingled from the contact with his lips and she jerked her hand back, curling her fingers into her palm. She closed her eyes and forced herself to focus on that night. "Mara was determined to put the trouble at the stables out of her mind for a while. She just wanted to have some fun, and she wanted me to enjoy myself, too. So we went to that party at Skip's frat house."

"Was it fun?" he asked.

She released a shaky sigh. "I don't know. I don't remember much of that night. I know I couldn't stop thinking about a test I had the next day, and I wanted to go back to our apartment and study. But I knew Mara was upset about what she'd seen at the stables, so I didn't want to leave her in case she needed me." Tears stung her eyes and made her nose tingle. "But then I had a drink…and it hit me so hard."

"You weren't yet twenty-one," he said.

She wasn't surprised that a former Marine MP and the current head of campus security would point that out. She and Mara had both been just twenty when

Mara died. "I know twenty-one is the legal drinking age here."

"Probably not in some of the countries where you grew up, though."

She shrugged. "I don't know. I hadn't had a drink of alcohol before that night." Or since. "That's probably why it hit me so hard. I remember dancing with Mara, but we always danced. So I'm not sure if I'm remembering that night or all the times we danced around our apartment." Her heart ached with missing her best friend—the best friend she'd ever had—and the pain was so intense now that she pressed a hand to her chest.

"You don't have to do this," Ryder said. "You can stop there."

"I wish I had. I wish none of the rest of it happened."

He sucked in a breath as if bracing himself, then asked, "*What* happened?"

"After that drink there was music and lights and laughter…and then I woke up in a strange bedroom. I was wearing a man's T-shirt and sweatpants…"

A muscle twitched in Ryder's cheek as if he was clenching his jaw. "Skip's." The name came through his gritted teeth like he was spitting out used tobacco.

She nodded. "But he just loaned me his clothes after I got sick all over mine. And he gave me his bed, too, and slept on the floor next to me with a bucket, in case I got sick again."

"How do you know that?" Ryder asked, his blue eyes narrowed with skepticism.

"Did you not hear me? I woke up in his bed." And she felt sick again, admitting what a fool she'd been.

"But you don't remember that night, so *he* must have been the one who told you what happened," Ryder said. "Just like how he told you I'm not related to Mara."

She shook her head. "But Amy Towers and Gretchen Manchester backed up his story." And had hounded her that entire last year of college over what a fool she'd made of herself, over how she'd betrayed her best friend. "And all his frat brothers in the house knew that he was taking care of me all night while I kept getting sick. He couldn't have killed Mara. He's not the bad man you think he is."

"But the texts and the letters he sent her…"

"Mara just laughed at them," Kristy shared. "She said it just showed how immature he was. That was why she liked…"

"What?" Ryder asked when she trailed off. "What did she like?"

"Someone older," Kristy replied.

Ryder's cheek twitched again. And this time another name slipped through his gritted teeth, "Dean…"

"She liked him," Kristy agreed. The way Mara had talked about him, with such excitement and affection, it had been more than like, but Kristy didn't want to upset Ryder anymore. But there was more. "Do you want me to go on? To tell you about what happened after I woke up that morning?" Her stomach churned at the thought of reliving that nightmare, especially with someone who'd loved Mara like Ryder had.

Maybe he dreaded hearing about when Kristy had found his sister because he said, "You can stop there. I know the rest. It's in the campus report and in state police records."

She shuddered at the memory of that morning. "But is it *all* there? If it was, why would someone be worried about me being back—so worried that they took shots at me tonight? There must be something else."

"Maybe it's what you told me earlier—what Skip reminded you about," Ryder said. "There was no mention of the kid stealing ketamine in that report, and there was nothing about Dean."

"I only know what my statement was for the report. When the police got to the apartment, after campus security had called them, they separated me and Skip before they interviewed us," she said, grimacing as she remembered how the police had treated them. "Like they thought either one or both of us might have done that." She nearly gagged on the notion of anyone believing she could have intentionally hurt Mara, let alone viciously stab her.

"How did Skip happen to be there with you?" Ryder asked. And it was clear he still considered Mara's boyfriend his number one suspect.

Had he ever suspected her, too? Like those troopers had seemed to at first?

"After I woke up in his room, Skip insisted on walking me back to my apartment to help smooth things over between me and Mara. I didn't know what he was talking about—I couldn't remember—but he explained that I had hit on him and Mara saw it and got upset and ran out of the party. That's how I got left there—why I was in his bed—because I put myself there." Her face heated with utter humiliation rushing over her, and her stomach roiled. Fortunately it was empty or she might have thrown up like she had that night. She closed her eyes now, unable to bear how Ryder was probably looking at her, like he had that day of the memorial service…with disgust.

Tears leaked out from beneath her closed lids and streaked down her cheeks. She forced herself to continue. "I told Skip he'd already cleaned up enough of the mess I'd made, and that I would go inside alone to talk to Mara. But when I opened the door and I saw the place trashed and the blood and Mara…" Her throat burned even now from her cries. "Skip rushed inside to see why I was screaming, and he tried to help her. I just froze there, hysterical, but he tried… even though it was already too late."

"She died hours before."

"And I wasn't there," Kristy whispered, and she squeezed her eyes more tightly closed, unable to look at him, to see the recrimination she'd seen all those years ago at the memorial. "If I'd been there, she might not have died."

"Or you might have been murdered, too," Ryder said, and he touched her cheek, his fingers shaking slightly.

She opened her eyes and stared up into his handsome face, and she marveled that all she saw in his vivid blue eyes was concern.

He continued, "Just like someone is trying to kill you now."

She shook her head. "I don't think they're trying to kill me, just scare me away with the note on the mirror and..."

"The shove on the stairs?"

"The stairwell was crowded, so that might have been an accident...or just a warning to watch my step."

"Not that hard a shove," Ryder said. "You hit your head. You were unconscious and could have died. And just hours ago someone shot at you—"

"At my car," she maintained.

"And you lost control and went in the ditch," he said. "It could have been much more serious if you'd hit a tree or power pole instead."

"It still might have been just another warning."

"One you need to heed," he said.

She sighed. "Well, I can't leave now. Not with a smashed-up car." Fortunately she had insurance, but she imagined it would take a while to fix if the insurance authorized that; they might decide to total it if the cost of repairs exceeded the value. "But even if I could leave, I'm not going to. I'm staying at least until we find Mara's killer."

"I'm more worried that he's found you," Ryder said. "And he's going to keep trying to get rid of you."

"Just like you are?" she asked, but she smiled slightly to show she was teasing.

Ryder's face remained tense, with that telltale twitch of tension in his cheek. "I wish I never brought you here."

She flinched at a jab of pain, wondering if his regret was just because she was in danger. Or was there another reason he wished she hadn't come back? Before she could summon the courage to ask him, he was whisking her out to his truck and driving her back to her apartment. When they stepped out into the parking lot, a sudden chill raced over her, and it wasn't just the night breeze. It was that feeling…

Even though she could see nothing beyond the parking lot but shadows, she knew someone was out there, in the dark, watching them.

Had the shooter followed them onto campus?

Was he going to try for them again?

## Chapter Thirteen

The first light of day streaked through the blinds on the window of the faculty apartment where Ryder had been staying to make sure nothing happened to Kristy. He squinted against the sunlight and uttered a prayer of thanks that he'd survived the night. Those last shots had come unsettlingly close…when the gun had been fired at him and Kristy on the road between the Holdren estate and campus.

Last night, as he'd walked her to the faculty apartment building, he'd had an uneasy feeling that someone might try to shoot at them again. The creepy sensation between his shoulder blades had made him think someone was watching them from the shadows. But maybe he was just paranoid after everything that had happened since Kristy's arrival on campus.

He'd managed to get her to her apartment with nothing else happening. And he'd even resisted the urge to give her another hug before he'd closed the door between them. She was beating herself up for not saving his sister, and now he was beating himself up for being so harsh with her and for bringing her back here just to break Skip's alibi.

But she hadn't broken his alibi. She hadn't convinced Ryder that he was wrong about the man either. By her own admission, she didn't remember much about that night, so how could she be so sure that he hadn't left her? That Skip hadn't slipped out, killed Mara and then returned to his room? Ryder intended to follow up with the frat brothers and with Amy and Gretchen and see if they still confirmed his alibi.

And if they did…

Then Ryder would have to admit he was wrong. Apparently there was a lot he hadn't known that had been going on with his little sister. He hadn't known how Mara had felt about Dean—about her crush on him. He hadn't known about her catching the kid stealing ketamine in the stables. He hadn't known his little sister nearly as well as he'd thought he had.

As Kristy Kendall had.

But he knew someone else who'd known her well, probably even better than Kristy. And certainly better than he had. He reached for the phone he'd left charging on the bedside table, and he called a familiar number. Home.

"Good morning, sweetheart," his stepmom greeted him cheerfully.

And he grimaced as he saw the time. Six in Michigan meant five in Austin. "I'm sorry I called so early," he apologized. "I didn't realize what time it was."

"It's fine," she assured him. "You know how early your father gets up."

"Is he already gone?"

"Just heading out the door now," she said. "He says hi."

Ryder doubted that; his father hardly talked at all anymore. After losing Mara, he lost himself working on the ranch. Ryder understood; he'd done the same thing with the rodeo until Dean had offered him this job. He'd thought the offer had been out of friendship, but now he wondered...

He wondered about everything.

"How are you?" he asked her.

"I'm good, honey," she replied. "I'm good."

She was good, through and through, and she deserved happiness. But it had been stolen from her when Mara had been taken away. Becky persisted in acting cheerful, in being positive, but Ryder could hear the hollowness to her happiness. She was just acting.

That was why, over the past ten years, he hadn't often done what he was about to do: talk to her about Mara. "I'm sorry."

"I told you it's fine," she said. "We've been awake for nearly an hour."

"No," he said. "I'm sorry about Mara."

"You had nothing to do with that, Ryder," she said. "A horrible thing happened, and there was no way you could have predicted it and no way you could have protected her. You need to stop blaming yourself."

He didn't think he was the only one who blamed

him. Ever since Ryder had brought Mara's body home to bury, his father hadn't looked at him…as if he couldn't bear the sight of him.

First Mama and then Mara…the losses were too great to bear. So Ryder understood that his father's feelings were all over the place. His were, too. And he had no idea how his stepmother really felt; maybe Becky was happy. Maybe somehow, in her deep faith, she'd found the acceptance and the peace that eluded Ryder. The only way he would get any closure would be after he found and brought to justice the person who'd killed his baby sister.

"I found Kristy Kendall," he said.

His stepmother audibly sucked in a breath, then replied, "You need to stop blaming her, too."

"I thought she was lying to protect him. Now I don't know what the truth is."

"She's an honest girl, Ryder, a good girl," Mom said. Then she chuckled. "Woman now. When I think of her, I think of Mara's awkward and shy roommate. She was so sweet and spiritual. An introvert to Mara's extrovert. They were so good for each other."

"Were they?" he wondered aloud. "Because Mara didn't survive…"

His stepmom gasped. "Ryder, that's not Kristy's fault."

"That's not what she thinks," he shared.

"Oh, poor girl." Mom's voice cracked with tears. "That's terrible. Mara would be so upset…over both of you blaming yourselves."

"I don't think either of us will stop doing that until

we find out who really is to blame," he admitted, and as he did, he realized Kristy was right. They needed to work together to find Mara's killer. He would just have to work extra hard to keep Kristy safe while they did it.

"You need to be careful, sweetheart," she said with concern. "Hopefully, though, that person has been put behind bars already for some other crimes, and he can't hurt anyone else."

Ryder might have believed that, too, since there had been no other murders on campus. Until Kristy had returned and she had nearly been murdered.

The killer was definitely still out there and entirely too close. Maybe even closer than Ryder had realized. "Mom, I have to ask you something."

"Anything, honey," she said with the instant generosity that had healed a little boy's broken heart all those years ago.

That was why he'd started calling her Mom even though she'd told him he didn't have to—that he could keep calling her Becky. But when his baby sister was born, he hadn't wanted her to call her mother Becky, so he'd started calling Becky Mom. And somehow he knew that his mother, whom he'd always called Mama, wouldn't have minded a bit. He just now realized he'd gotten something else wrong with Kristy.

When he'd told her that Mara had reminded him that there was still good in the world…

It wasn't Mara who'd reminded him; it was Mom.

"What is it?" she asked.

He had to clear his throat of all the emotion choking him before he could reply. "I need you to tell me about Mara." He felt bad for asking, for putting her through this, but to his surprise, she laughed. "I was worried about upsetting you."

"It upsets me more to not talk about her," she said. "I don't want to forget any detail about my daughter."

Tears rushed to his eyes, and he had to squeeze them shut for a moment, fighting to hold them back. "It's not too hard?"

"It's hard that she's gone, and that's why I want to remember every moment of when she was here," she explained.

He wondered if his dad let her talk about Mara, or if he acted the way he had when Ryder's mother died—like it was too painful to bring up. Ever.

Ryder understood because it hurt him so much, too, to think about either of them. But maybe he could take comfort, like Mom did, in the memories.

"Tell me about your daughter then," he said.

"Your sister," she said, and he could hear the smile in her voice.

"I know my sister," he said. "I didn't know her as a friend until I talked to Kristy. And now I want to know her as your daughter. You two were so close."

"Twins—that's what your daddy called us," she said. "That's how Mara introduced me when I visited her on campus."

"You were here..."

"Several times," she said.

He'd never found the time, had always been so busy, and that was a regret he would always have.

Maybe if he'd visited, he might have seen the threat… the danger to Mara. Guilt weighed heavily on his shoulders and his heart.

"That's how I know how good Mara and Kristy were for each other," she said. "Mara got Kristy to be social and fun. And Kristy got Mara to be more thoughtful and careful."

"Not careful enough…"

"There are some dangers you can't see until it's too late," she said.

"What about Dean?" he asked.

"What *about* Dean?" The smile left her voice now. And Ryder's blood chilled. "What was going on with him and Mara?"

"He's married."

"Not anymore," Ryder said.

"But he was then," Mom said, disapproval sharpening her sweet voice a bit. "I had to remind your sister of that a few times. She liked flirting with him. Too much…and he liked flirting back…too much."

Ryder's heart pounded a little harder. So there had been some truth to what Skip had told Kristy. At least about Dean.

"Do you think they ever crossed a line?"

"I don't think so," Mom said.

"But would she have told you if she had?"

"She would have told me before she would have told Kristy," Mom said. "That must be why you're calling me—because Kristy didn't know. Mara was well aware that Kristy didn't approve of the flirting."

"I doubt Dean's wife would have either," he said.

And if she'd found out, she probably would have divorced Dean much sooner. But something else struck him about what Mom said. "If Kristy wouldn't have approved of that, would she have ever flirted with Skip Holdren when he was going out with her best friend?"

His mother sucked in a breath. "Definitely not. I don't think she even liked him, and Kristy is one of those people who tries to see the good in everyone."

Ryder certainly hadn't shown her much good in himself yet. "You know she's his alibi for that night," he said.

She released a breath now in a shaky sigh. "I never understood that."

"She says she got drunk and was hitting on Skip, and Mara got mad and left her at the frat party and went back to their apartment alone."

"No."

"What do you mean no?"

"None of that would have happened," Mom said. "Kristy wouldn't have gotten drunk—"

"She admitted to having a drink."

Mom sighed. "So Mara finally talked her into trying it? In the two years they'd known each other, she hadn't managed that."

"Mara drank? Underaged?"

Mom laughed. "Oh, Ryder, she wasn't as perfect as you thought she was. She was a good person, though. And another thing I can tell you about that night is that she would have never gotten mad at Kristy and left her anywhere, especially not if the girl was drunk.

There's no way Mara would have abandoned her best friend." She paused for a moment, her breathing a little shaky as if she was struggling with emotion. "And if she did, then Kristy shouldn't feel guilty at all about what happened. In fact it's amazing something didn't happen to her as well."

Ryder felt a sharp jab to his heart thinking of what could have happened to Kristy, of a world without her in it. She was so beautiful…inside as much as out.

"No," Mom said sharply again. "I just can't believe Mara would have left her there. She loved her too much. They were like sisters as much as friends."

And he finally understood why Kristy was so determined to find Mara's killer despite the threats on her life; she missed Mara as much as he did. She'd loved her, too.

So despite what Skip had filled in for Kristy about that night of which she remembered so little, there was still so much left out. So much that didn't make sense. So much that he and Kristy needed to figure out before the killer could try again.

Kristy had had a shadow all day. First Ryder. He'd taken her from her apartment door to the lecture hall where she had a class. He'd even sat through part of that class before another campus security guard had taken his place. And now that guard was walking her to the administration building where she had a meeting with Dean. She would have told the young security guard that his protection wasn't necessary, but she couldn't lie.

Not even to herself anymore…

Maybe the push on the stairs and the gunshots had been meant only as threats, but either time Kristy could have died. Probably would have died if not for Ryder's interference and protection. So when the young man walked her into the empty reception area of the provost's office, she heartily thanked him for his escort. He left her with a smile, and when she heard his boss's voice drifting from beneath the closed door of Dean's office, she realized why he was leaving. He was handing her back to his boss.

What was Ryder doing here?

She was the one who'd been asked to attend this meeting with the provost. Dean's voice drifted out from beneath the door now. "I'm not going to fire her. So many students have been trying to get into her classes that I'm going to ask her if she has time to fit in another one this semester."

So that was the reason he'd asked her to meet him here, not to terminate her employment like she'd feared when she'd received his email with the meeting request. Like Ryder was apparently still trying to get Dean to do despite his agreeing that they should work together to find Mara's murderer. She found it hard to breathe with the sudden pressure on her chest, on her heart.

"I'm not trying to get her fired," Ryder said.

And that pressure on her chest eased somewhat.

"That's good," Dean said. "Because I wouldn't do it, even for you. The students are really responding to how she teaches. I feel like they're going to learn a lot from her."

"I already did," Ryder said.

"Did you sit in on another one of her classes?" Dean asked.

"As a matter-of-fact—"

"Ms. Kendall," the receptionist loudly exclaimed as she walked into the reception area. "I'll let the provost know you're here."

But the men must have heard her because the door to Dean's office opened, and he gestured her inside. "Kristy," he said. "I hope I haven't kept you waiting. I wasn't expecting Ryder's visit today." And clearly he didn't welcome it. He turned toward his old friend whose long, lean body lounged in one of the chairs in front of the provost's desk. "We're going to have to finish this discussion another time, Ryder."

But Ryder didn't take the hint to get up and leave. Instead he pushed his cowboy hat back a bit on his head and focused an intense stare on Dean. "No, it's already nearly ten years overdue."

Dean returned Ryder's stare, his dark eyes narrowed. "What are you talking about?"

"You and my sister," Ryder said. "How far did the flirting between the two of you go? Far enough to cost you your marriage and probably your job, too?"

Dean slammed his door shut and stalked over to his friend. He leaned over his chair, his face close to Ryder's, and yelled, "How dare you!"

"How dare you cross the line with any student

but most especially my sister!" Ryder bellowed back at him.

"Please!" Kristy beseeched them. "Calm down. Let's talk about this rationally."

But neither man heard her as they continued to glare at each other, faces inches apart. "You must have lost your mind to come in here and make these kinds of accusations!" Dean said, his body shaking with outrage.

Ryder narrowed his eyes and studied Dean with blatant suspicion. "Interesting that you haven't answered my question yet. You just keep deflecting."

"Because such a ridiculous, insulting question doesn't deserve a response," he replied. "And I'm not sure you deserve my friendship. Skip Holdren has been after me ever since I hired you, to fire you. I thought it was because he didn't want you to find proof of his guilt, so I didn't care that I was antagonizing a major St. Michel's benefactor and risking my own career. I cared about you, about your quest for justice. If you can't see that I'm your friend—"

"Stop," Kristy interrupted. "It was my fault. I'm the one who told him about Mara's crush and that Skip suggested it was more than that. Ryder never doubted you until I made him doubt you."

"Then maybe he's right," Dean said, and he whirled toward her with all his outrage. "Maybe you're the one I should fire."

Ryder jumped up from his chair then and stepped between them. "You just said more kids were signing up for her class."

Despite the tension in the room, Kristy felt a flash of pride again. She hadn't even graded anything yet, so students weren't signing up because they thought the class was easy. They were signing up for *her*.

"And you're not the only one Skip threw under the bus," Ryder told Dean. "He talked about Joe Campbell and his kid, too, about some stolen ketamine. Mara saw Joe's kid steal it from the vet at the stable."

Dean sighed. "I knew that Joe's kid was getting drugs from somewhere and selling them on campus. Joe knew, too, but he didn't do anything to punish or to even stop his kid. That's why I fired him."

"I thought he retired."

"That's the choice he took," Dean said. "I didn't know it had been going on that long, though."

"There was nothing about it in any of Joe's records that I went through," Ryder said. "Not that he left a lot behind for me to go through. Now I know why."

Dean shrugged. "If someone had reported it, I doubt Joe would have written it up or let any of his team write it up. It was pretty clear he had been doing everything he could to protect his son."

*Would he have killed for him?* Kristy couldn't remember when Mara had left that party. What if she'd gone to Joe then to report his son? It might not have been too late; the party had started early in the afternoon since there had been no classes that day.

If only she could remember more…

But maybe she'd remembered too much, because telling Ryder about Mara's crush on Dean had caused so much tension between the friends. They kept glaring at each other. Before she could think of anything to smooth it over, the receptionist interrupted with an urgent call for the provost. She and Ryder walked out of his office, through the busy reception area and down the hall. When they stepped into the stairwell, Ryder clasped her arm and held her as they descended every step together, as if he was worried that someone would try to shove her down again.

She waited until they were in the parking lot and apologized. "I'm sorry," she said. "I didn't mean to cause problems between you."

He shook his head. "*You* didn't." He sighed. "And I know better than to lose my temper like that. If I would have questioned him calmly, maybe he wouldn't have gotten so defensive. But after talking to my stepmom this morning—"

"You talked to Becky? How is she?" Kristy's parents were warm, loving, selfless people, but Becky Lewis might have been even more so than the missionaries.

"She's…" His voice got gruff. "She's amazing."

"She and Mara were so close," Kristy said. "They were best friends."

"Like you and Mara," he said. "That's what Mom said about the two of you. That you were such good friends that…" His voice trailed off again but not with gruffness. He tensed and stared around them, his hand reaching beneath his jacket, probably for his holster. "Let's get in the truck."

And then she knew she wasn't the only one who kept having that weird sensation of being watched.

As Ryder opened the passenger's door for her, she glanced back at the administration building and noticed Dean in his office window staring down at them. She shivered and murmured, "He never answered you…about him and Mara."

Ryder glanced over his shoulder at the building, and that muscle twitched just above his tightly clenched jaw. He'd already pointed out to her that his friend had been defensive and had deflected Ryder's questions.

Kristy could think of only one reason Dean would do that: because he had something to hide. And how desperate was he to keep that hidden?

## Chapter Fourteen

Was it just Dean staring at them that had given Ryder that uneasy feeling? Or was there someone else out there? Like there'd been when she'd left Holdren's estate the night before?

But it wasn't dark now, and Ryder could see clearly...that he didn't know his friend as well as he'd thought he had. That what Ryder had considered harmless flirting might have been so much more.

And really there was no such thing as *harmless* flirting when a person was married to someone else and dealing with a student over whom they have power.

Ryder probably needed to go the president of the college, but he wasn't sure Wilson Montgomery was even fully functioning anymore. While he made appearances at the parties his wife threw for fundraising, he barely spoke to anyone.

Which meant that there was no one to monitor or question Dean's behavior...especially if he followed through on his threat to fire Ryder. After closing the passenger's door for Kristy, Ryder hurried around the front of the truck to the driver's side, but before he got inside, he glanced up at Dean's office window again. The guy was gone. Had he just sat back down at his desk? Or had he left his office entirely?

Ryder hopped into the truck and started the engine. Then he turned toward Kristy. "Where do you need to be? Do you have another class?"

"No, I don't. And I think we should try to talk to Joe Campbell now," she said. "Find out where his son is these days." Her eyes narrowed behind her lenses, though, almost as if she had some idea where that might be.

It should have been prison, and probably would have been had his father not intervened and covered up for him. How far had he gone to do that?

"*I'm* going to talk to Joe Campbell," he said. "I just want to know where to drop you off and have Brad take over for me."

"I'm going with you," she said.

He glanced across the console at her. "Kristy, that's not a good idea. I know Joe pretty well. I talked to him regularly on the phone for years after Mara's death, checking to see if he or the state police got any closer to identifying a suspect." Actually, he'd wanted to know if they'd found a way to break Skip's alibi. But that had never happened.

What if Skip was innocent and it had been some-one else, someone Ryder thought he could trust? Maybe Joe would know something about that—something about Dean and Mara, too. If Joe was anything like Ryder was, some of the students might have come to him…like they came to Ryder. Might have confided in him, too.

He continued, "And since I've been living in Eagle Valley, Joe and I have gone fishing quite a few times. He'll talk more openly to me than he will to you."

"He was sweet to me…after I found Mara," she said. "I had to stay another year to finish earning credits for my degree, and not many people were nice to me then. They'd heard I was Skip's alibi and thought I'd betrayed her."

Ryder's heart ached for how alone she must have felt with her best friend gone and nobody around to comfort her.

"But Joe Campbell was nice to me," she continued, "and Dean and Pastor Howard and… Skip."

And really any one of them could have killed Mara.

That realization staggered Ryder even more than suddenly suspecting a friend. Kristy had been here alone for that year after Mara died. She could have easily become the killer's next victim. If he'd been worried then like he seemed to be worried now, that she might remember something.

Or was it the combination of her being back while Ryder was here? Maybe it was working together that was putting her in danger. Because the killer realized that Ryder would figure out what she must have forgotten….

His head began to pound like he had the concussion she had. "If you don't have a class to teach or papers to grade—"

"I don't," she interjected. "Classes just started. There are no assignments due for a while. So this is the perfect time for me to help you investigate."

He shook his head. "This is the perfect time for you to get some rest. You've been through a lot since your return here." Too much.

And that was all his fault. He never should have manipulated her into coming back to St. Michel's.

"I won't be able to rest until I finally learn the truth," she said. "And maybe seeing Joe again will help me remember more, like seeing Skip did."

But had she remembered or had Skip planted those memories?

Maybe Joe could help shed some light on that, if he didn't get defensive and deflect his questions like Dean had. "Okay," Ryder relented, but he wasn't sure she would have given him a choice.

Kristy was tougher than he'd thought. Those threats to her life hadn't scared her off like the killer must have believed they would; they'd made her even more determined to find out the truth.

He glanced across the console at her. She wore black slacks today, like she had yesterday, with a light pink sweater. There was more color in the sweater than in her face, which was pale, but for the dark circles beneath her eyes. She really needed to rest, but he understood her determination to finally find out the truth.

"Joe's place isn't far from campus," he said. "He

has a cabin near a creek in the valley. There's good fishing in that creek." He'd enjoyed the time he'd spent with the former chief of campus security. Just like Dean, he'd considered the older man a friend.

And Joe appeared to consider him the same when, moments later, he answered Ryder's knock at his door with a grin. "My successor," he said and reached through the open door to heartily shake Ryder's hand. Then he glanced at Kristy who stood beside him. "Miss..."

"Kendall," she said. "Kristy Kendall."

The smile slipped off Joe's face then. Her name obviously affected him. "I know," he said quietly. "I remember you." But yet he'd hesitated to say her name, as if he was so troubled about seeing her again that he hadn't been able to utter it.

She smiled at him. "I remember you. You were very kind."

That was what Ryder had always thought of him, too. But he hadn't known about his kid, about his cover-up. "I hope you don't mind that I brought Kristy along with me. She's back on campus now, teaching a creative writing course."

Joe summoned his smile again. "I'm not surprised."

"You saw it in the alumni newsletter?" Ryder asked. Why had Dean included that? Because she was an alum, or because he'd wanted to spread suspicion around when those threats were made against her?

Joe glanced at him through slightly narrowed eyes. "Well, yeah, but I was talking about how she was always scribbling in some notebook—" he turned back to her then and added "—when you weren't at the church."

"You spent some time in that church, too," she said.

"What were you praying for, Joe?" Ryder asked. "Forgiveness?"

Joe furrowed his brow entirely now, adding more wrinkles to his already heavily lined face. He pushed a slightly shaking hand through his gray hair. "For patience. Something you've always had short supply of, Ryder. What are you doing here? I don't think you brought Miss Kendall here to check out our fishing spot."

"I've been more than patient," Ryder said. "Soon it's going to be ten years since Mara was murdered. And her killer has never been caught. And I have to wonder how hard anyone ever looked for him."

"You'd have to ask the state police about that," Joe said. "They took over the investigation. I was out of my league with a murder."

"What about with a kid stealing and selling drugs on campus?" Ryder asked. "Were you out of your league with that, too? Is that why you never turned your son in?"

Joe groaned and staggered back a bit, clutching the doorframe.

Kristy rushed forward and reached out to steady him. "Are you okay, Mr. Campbell?" she asked with concern.

He nodded and stepped out onto the porch where

he'd left them standing. He sank into one of the rocking chairs teetering in the breeze. "Dean told you about Joey?"

"Mara told me," Kristy said. "She told me ten years ago that she saw him stealing from the vet at the stables. She was going to report him."

"But she never got the chance," Ryder remarked. "Someone killed her first."

Joe glanced up at him. "And you were always so convinced it was Skip Holdren. Why are you looking at my Joey now? He was just a dumb kid then, desperate to be popular despite nobody trusting him because his dad was the campus top cop. He wouldn't have hurt anyone. He just wanted to fit in."

"Sometimes we're too close to someone to see what they're really capable of," Ryder remarked. "I recently learned that myself."

"If you're talking about your sister, you're wrong," Joe said. "Mara was a good girl, like Miss Kendall here."

"I wasn't talking about Mara. I'm talking about Dean."

Joe chuckled, but it sounded sharp with bitterness. "Dean Stolz. He's a lot like Joey. Just wants to be popular, but he's always been a whole lot smarter than my boy has ever been."

"Where is Joey now?" Ryder asked. "I'd like to talk to him."

Joe shrugged. "You're wasting your time, but then I guess it's your time to waste."

"I might have wasted ten years looking at the wrong suspect," Ryder admitted.

"Skip Holdren."

"Yeah."

"That's where Joey is," Joe said. "Wherever Skip is."

Kristy gasped, reached out for Ryder now and grasped his arm. "I thought I saw him last night at the estate. He was leaving and let me in."

So Joey had seen her there. With as little as Kristy had changed over the past ten years, he had probably recognized her. And maybe he had waited until she left and shot out her tires...

"Does Joey have a gun?" Ryder asked.

Joe shook his head. "No. And like I said, he would never hurt anyone."

"Drugs hurt," Ryder said. "You know that. You know how many kids get hooked and OD on them. And here your own kid was dealing them."

"He wasn't the only one," Joe said. "GHB and ro-hypnol have always been rampant on campus. That was probably what Miss Kendall was slipped that night—why she forgot so much of it."

Of course. Being drugged would explain her memory loss and negate her credibility to be a true alibi for Skip. But with other possible suspects, Ryder wasn't sure Skip needed an alibi. "Did you have her tested for it?" he asked. "Was it in her system?"

"I had a nurse give her a physical that morning, but by the time she took the blood test, it was too late for anything to be detected. At least nobody had taken advantage of her while she'd been incapacitated."

Mom was right. There was no way Mara would have abandoned Kristy in that condition. Before she'd left for college, Ryder had gone over and over with her all the dangers that could happen to young girls on college campuses. He'd always told her to stick together, never go off by herself or let a friend do that either.

"I wasn't hurt," Kristy said. "Mara was the one who was—who was murdered."

Joe's face flushed, and he looked almost guiltily at Ryder. "Yeah, that was a tragedy."

"A tragedy that's been compounded with every year that passes that her murder goes unsolved," Ryder said. He could not let another year pass without justice.

"Was there anything else, Mr. Campbell?" Kristy asked. "Anything that you saw or heard about from that night?"

Joe's brow furrowed again. "A strange report did come in. Someone saying they saw a guy carrying a woman along one of the paths near the campus apartments."

"But Mara was murdered in our apartment," Kristy said. "Nobody carried her anywhere."

"Not her," Ryder said as he began to piece together what might have happened that night...

Kristy stared through the rain-streaked windshield of Ryder's truck as he drove farther away from campus. Just like when she'd left Skip's, she was reeling from what she'd learned, from the notes that Joe Campbell had kept about Mara's murder…notes that she and Ryder had gone over with him.

"It doesn't make sense," she said. None of it did. There had been no reason for anyone to murder someone as good and pure as Mara had been. "Why are we going to talk to this witness? That can't have anything to do with what happened that night…"

"Because it doesn't make sense," Ryder said. "It's too much of a coincidence that something like that, someone carrying an unconscious woman, was witnessed on the same night Mara died."

"She died in our apartment," Kristy said. "She was not murdered somewhere else and carried there. There were signs of a struggle." She shuddered as she remembered the blood. The holes in the wall in the kitchen. The drawers pulled all the way out, their contents strewn across the floor.

"I still have questions."

He'd already tried asking them over the phone, after calling the number Joe had had for the witness, Tyler Milanowski. The number, for a cell that the witness still owned, wasn't all Joe had had in the records he'd brought home after retiring. He'd had copies of witness statements and, even though she'd refused to look at them, crime scene photos. Kristy suspected Ryder wasn't the only one still working to close Mara's murder case. Despite Joe's claims of turning over the investigation to the state police, he still wanted to know what had happened to Mara and who was responsible.

Was he worried that it could be his son? Kristy was. And that was who they should be talking to. Not this witness.

While Tyler Milanowski had answered the call, he hadn't understood what Ryder was asking. That must have been due to the poor cell reception in the area, though, since he'd given his address to Ryder so they could talk to him in person. After graduating from St. Michel's, he'd stayed in the area, settling into one of the new condo complexes in Eagle Valley.

And that was where they were heading now.

This just felt like a waste of time to Kristy. "We should be talking to Joey," she said.

"*I* will," Ryder said.

"Oh." So Ryder also knew this was a waste of time, of her time. He fully intended to follow up on the real lead without her.

"He might be the one who shot at you last night—"

"At you, too!" she exclaimed.

"And that's why it will be smart to have a trooper go with me when I talk to Joey," he said.

"Oh."

"Does *that* make sense?" he asked, and his mouth curved into a slight grin as if he was teasing her.

"Yes," she begrudgingly admitted. She didn't want to get shot at again. Once had been more than enough. But she didn't want him or a trooper getting shot at either.

"You're already in too much danger," Ryder said.

"I'm not knowingly going to put you in any more." He took one hand from the steering wheel and reached across the console to squeeze hers.

Her pulse quickened with the contact. Did Ryder care about her? Or was it just that he was a natural protector, after what he'd gone through with losing his mom and then his sister? She shouldn't take it personally or imagine anything personal ever developing between them. The only thing they had in common was Mara and losing her.

There was no way something good could come of that tragedy. And Kristy didn't believe she deserved anything good anyway, not after she'd failed the best friend she'd ever had. If only she had been there for Mara.

"You're not the one who pushed me down the stairs or shot at me," she said. "You're not putting me in danger." But he was dangerous to her; he made her wish for things she didn't deserve to have. Like love.

"I orchestrated your return to St. Michel's," he said. "And having you come with me here was probably a mistake too." He returned his hand to the steering wheel to turn onto a residential road. "This is it."

This development wasn't like the condominium complexes she'd seen in the cities where she'd lived over the past nine years. Instead of town houses or single-story attached units, this one had individual home buildings with space between them and mature trees towering over them. "This must have been here awhile," she remarked.

Ryder nodded. "I think it's one of Skip's dad's

properties. His company is responsible for many of the new developments around Eagle Valley. He moved away, but he still runs it. Guess he doesn't trust it to Skip."

"So you're not the only one who doesn't trust him?"

Ryder parked the truck, but he didn't get out. Instead he turned toward her. "Why do you?" he asked. "You can't remember enough of that night to be sure he didn't leave you alone in his room and go back to yours and Mara's apartment."

"But his frat brothers and Amy and Gretchen backed up his alibi, too." Would they have lied for him, though? She always tried to see the good in people, and it was hard for her to consider that many people might have lied to protect a killer. It didn't make sense.

"Were they there?" he asked. "Were they in that room with you two? Is there any way that anyone but the two of you would know for certain if he was there the entire time?"

She swallowed hard on the sudden rush of dread. Was Ryder right? Had she been protecting the wrong person all these years?

"Even Joe thinks someone drugged you. He had the results of your blood work in that box of old records too."

"He said it didn't show rohypnol or GHB," she reminded him.

"No, but it didn't show alcohol either," he said. "You weren't drunk that night, Kristy."

The weight of guilt she'd been carrying for so long

lifted a little. So someone had slipped something in that drink.

But it hadn't even been hers.

"That wasn't my drink," she said.

He narrowed his eyes and asked, "Was it Mara's?"

She nodded.

"Mom pointed out something to me this morning that you need to know. Mara wouldn't have gotten mad at you for flirting with Skip—if that even really happened. And she certainly wouldn't have left you anywhere if she thought you were drunk or incapacitated."

Kristy sucked in a breath with the realization that he was right. He had to be. The Mara she'd known, the best friend who'd protected her from the campus mean girls, wouldn't have left Kristy alone. She felt a twinge of guilt that she'd ever considered that she would. But everyone else had supported Skip's claim that Mara had gotten mad at Kristy and left her. "So what really happened that night?"

Ryder opened his mouth, but she couldn't hear what he said because there was a gunshot blast. And the back window of the truck shattered. Glass flew all over the seat and the console, along with droplets of blood.

Fear gripped her, squeezing her heart so tightly that she barely managed to scream. And she focused on praying, "Please God, please protect us."

*Please don't let Ryder die.*

## Chapter Fifteen

Shards of glass sparkled like diamonds in Kristy's hair. "Thank you, God," Ryder fervently declared. *Thank you, God, that she didn't get hit.*

"You're bleeding," she murmured, and her fingertips touched his cheek.

He flinched at a jolt of pain and remembered the sharp sting against his skin when that window had first shattered moments ago. He'd managed to push Kristy below the windows and duck down himself as more shots rang out.

Someone must have been home in one of the condos because the police had been called, and they'd been close enough that the sirens had rung out almost immediately after those first shots.

"You have a piece of glass in that wound," she said. "You need to go to the hospital."

He shook his head and bits of glass fell from the brim of his cowboy hat onto the ground outside the truck. Ryder was blessed that he hadn't been hurt more than the little scratch on his cheek. "I'm fine."

He was just furious that he'd fallen for what must have been a setup. The trooper who'd arrived first on the scene was looking over the cab on the pickup now. At Ryder's urging, he'd already checked to see if Tyler Milanowski was home. He wasn't. But it was clear from the warm cup of coffee left on his kitchen table that he hadn't been gone long.

"What is the deal?" the trooper asked, the same one who'd taken their statement the night before. His brow furrowed, moving the brim of his tan hat as he peered up at Ryder. He was a bit shorter than him and younger with an earnest disposition. "Who's trying to kill you two and why?"

"You need to check out Tyler Milanowski," Ryder replied. "He was the one who told us to meet him here."

"When you said that's who you were coming to see, I ran him right away. The guy doesn't even have a parking ticket," the trooper replied. "Why would he take potshots at you and Miss Kendall? Do you know him?"

Ryder shook his head, and more shards of glass drifted to the asphalt. "No. We didn't get the chance to meet him."

And maybe someone had wanted to make sure they didn't have that opportunity. Who? Who would be worried about what Tyler might tell them? Or was that all the dead end that Kristy thought it was?

Had Joe Campbell put this in motion to protect his son?

He could have called ahead and had Joey get rid

of Tyler and lay in wait for them. Or Joe could have followed them himself. Or Dean...

Dean could have been following them the entire time. Ryder hadn't been paying close enough attention to the road. He'd let Kristy distract him. Her soft voice, her sweet scent, the kindness she radiated...

She was staring at him with such concern now, just over the small cut on his face. She was so empathetic that he was surprised she'd survived her years of traveling with her missionary parents and all she must have seen then. Or maybe that was what had made her so empathetic.

And why she carried such a weight on her shoulders that they bowed slightly with it. Or was that the guilt she felt over Mara's death? He bore the weight of that, too. And if something happened to Kristy, he'd carry an even heavier load. "Trooper Stevens, there are a couple of people I'd like you to meet and interview. A couple of people who knew or might have been informed that Miss Kendall and I were heading here to talk to Mr. Milanowski. I'd also like to sit in on these interviews if possible. But first I need to get one of my security guards from the college to come pick up and protect Miss Kendall."

"I want to go, too," Kristy said.

"I'm not sure I should bring along Mr. Lewis," the trooper said. "But he is campus security and has a criminal justice degree."

Obviously, Tyler Milanowski wasn't the only person on whom the thorough trooper had run a background check.

"I won't put you in danger, Miss Kendall. And if I could get the authorization, I'd be tempted to put you in police custody for your protection. Stuff like this doesn't happen around Eagle Valley. These shootings…"

They'd also told the trooper about the shove on the stairs, as well as the note left on the mirror in her first apartment on campus.

"Nothing this serious has happened since…" He trailed off.

"Since my sister died," Ryder finished for him.

The officer nodded. "I grew up in Eagle Valley and had just gotten my driver's license when that happened, and my mom made me drive my sisters everywhere and make sure nothing happened to them. It freaked everyone out back then, and it's still all anybody around here talks about." His dark eyes widened a bit with excitement. "It would be great to finally close that case."

And Ryder suspected the young trooper would like the credit for doing that. It would certainly help his career. Ryder didn't care what came of it, just that the case was finally closed and that justice was delivered without anyone else getting hurt.

Especially Kristy.

Getting the glass out of her hair hadn't been easy, but she'd done it. Getting the fear out of her heart and mind wouldn't be as easy. Over an hour after the shooting, she was still shaking with adrenaline and fear, but she was more afraid for Ryder, that he was putting himself in danger again. He and the trooper had been adamant she couldn't go with them, so there was only one thing she could do. With Brad, the security guard, shadowing her, she headed to St. Michel's little fieldstone church. And she was so deep in prayer that Pastor Howard's sudden appearance in front of her startled her into releasing a squeak of alarm.

Brad jumped as well, then chuckled. "Pastor Howard, you move fast for..." His face flushed bright red.

Pastor Howard chuckled. "For an old man? I'm probably not as old as you think I am, son." Then he turned toward Kristy. "Miss Kendall, I'm so happy to see you here."

"Kristy," she said. "You always called me Kristy before."

He smiled. "You're no longer a student. You're a professor now, dear."

"You're still a friend." One of the few she'd had after Mara died. She remembered what Ryder had said, about how Mara never would have left her there at a frat party when she was incapacitated. She had been Kristy's best friend, so there was no way that had happened.

She had to find out what really had. "And I'd love to talk to you right now, but I need to meet another friend," she said.

Except this woman had never been her friend. She hadn't even been Mara's because she'd been too envious of Mara's effervescent personality and her beauty and probably, especially, her riding skills. She hugged

Pastor Howard and then rushed from the church with Brad following close behind her.

Scrolling through old alumni newsletters on her phone gave her the contact information she needed, and, surprisingly, the woman agreed to meet her on campus, at the coffeehouse. She was tempted to call Ryder next, to let him know what she was doing as Brad drove her to the coffeehouse. But she figured Mara's old frenemy wouldn't speak as freely in front of the dead woman's brother as she would to Kristy. And he was busy…

Hopefully not getting shot at. And moments later when she took a seat at an outside table at the café, she closed her eyes and prayed as if she was still at the church.

*Please, God, keep Ryder safe. Please protect him from harm and release him from his guilt and regrets and sadness. And please, God, release me too if I deserve it…if I did nothing wrong.*

For so many years she'd blamed herself, thinking that she'd betrayed Mara. But she'd never been attracted to Skip. Even drugged, would she have flirted with him? She didn't know how to flirt now, and she was nearly thirty.

Because if she did know how, she would have started flirting with Ryder. He was the one she was attracted to…for his protectiveness, for his sense of responsibility, for his love of his family and honor and integrity. But his only interest in her was in helping find his sister's killer.

And she knew that neither of them would be able

to move on until Mara's murderer was caught. And when the killer was caught, then Ryder would no doubt return to the rodeo or his family ranch. There would be nothing for the cowboy in Eagle Valley once he got the justice he had sought for so long.

And her job was only temporary. When it was over, she had no idea what she'd do or where she'd go. She had some ideas for stories, and while she waited, she opened her notebook to jot down some notes about the story she most wanted to write.

*One about a little boy who witnesses his mother's murder and has to work hard to find the good in the world again.*

"You really haven't changed at all," a woman remarked.

Kristy looked up at Gretchen Manchester who loomed over the table as if she had just happened upon Kristy, as if she hadn't agreed to meet with her. "Please, sit down," Kristy implored her.

Gretchen glanced around her once, as if looking for someone.

Kristy had hoped she would come alone, but she should have guessed that Gretchen wouldn't go anywhere without Amy. She never had.

"Good," Gretchen murmured. "I don't recognize anyone." And she perched on the edge of the metal café chair opposite Kristy.

Apparently she just hadn't wanted to be seen with her. "You really haven't changed at all either," Kristy remarked.

And Gretchen smiled as if it was a compliment. To her, maybe it was.

But Kristy would prefer to have grown in maturity and wisdom than to have remained the same as she'd been ten years ago. Gretchen was right that Kristy hadn't changed—because she'd been stuck, carrying too heavy a load of guilt and regret to be able to move forward. Just like Ryder.

Hopefully he was getting some answers, but she wanted to help, too. And with Brad sitting at the next table over, watching them, she felt safe enough to handle this meeting on her own. But to get the real, honest answers she wanted, Kristy had to be stronger than she'd ever been, too. She had to be fierce like Mara had been when she'd protected her from Gretchen and Amy.

"I don't know why you called me and wanted to talk," Gretchen said. "You and I were never friends. And we will never be friends."

"No, we won't," Kristy agreed. "I don't want your friendship. I just want the truth. And an apology."

Gretchen made a muffled harrumphing noise and shook her head. "Wow, you're even weirder than you used to be. There's no way I'm ever apologizing to you."

"Not to me," Kristy said. "You owe an apology to Mara."

The color drained from Gretchen's face, and she fidgeted with her hands, which probably risked some damage since her nails were so long. "I don't know what you're talking about."

"I think you do," Kristy said. "I think you know what you did, how you lied and how Mara would have felt about it, about being maligned the way she has been."

Gretchen's dark eyes narrowed in a glare. "Nobody maligned Mara. You're the one who acted like a fool at that party, who got drunk, who hit on Skip. You're the one who betrayed your friend."

Kristy shook her head. "I saw the toxicology report."

Gretchen gasped then and clutched her hands so tightly that she snapped off one of her fake nails. But then she sucked in a breath and said, "So you were on drugs too that night?"

Kristy shook her head again. "No. The GHB or rohypnol was already out of my system, but so was the alcohol. Whatever I had to drink had moved through my system so quickly that blood alcohol didn't even register."

"Because you were throwing up."

"I don't doubt that," Kristy agreed. "But I doubt everything else." And her biggest regret was that she hadn't doubted it ten years ago, like Ryder had wanted her to do.

"Of course you would. You're trying to make yourself feel better."

Kristy laughed. "No, that's the one thing I haven't done all these years." She'd wallowed in her guilt, and that would have made Mara so mad. And channeling Mad Mara gave Kristy the strength to continue.

"How about you? How have you lived with yourself all these years?"

Gretchen made that harrumphing noise again, but it sounded choked, like she was struggling with something else. Her conscience?

Kristy hoped she had one. "Mara would have been so angry to know what you and Amy and Skip were saying...that she got mad at me, that she abandoned me when I was that out of it? She was my best friend and my fiercest protector. There is no way she would have left me in that condition at a frat party." And Kristy felt the guiltiest about thinking Mara would have done that.

Color returned to Gretchen's face now, flushing it a deep red. She didn't say anything, though.

So Kristy pressed on. "Ryder and Trooper Stevens are interviewing everyone from that night. I doubt that every one of Skip's frat brothers will lie for him like you and Amy have. And there was another witness..."

And the color receded again, leaving Gretchen ghostly pale and shaking. "Another witness?"

"Saw a man carrying a woman across campus."

Gretchen snorted then and her thin body relaxed a bit. "Mara carried you. And nobody would have mistaken her for a man. Well, I helped, too. You were passed out cold."

"So Mara didn't leave me there," she said. "She carried me home." Realizing what that meant, Kristy shivered with a sudden, cold dread. "So I was there when she was murdered."

Gretchen shook her head. "No, you must have woke up after Mara put you to bed. Then you snuck out and returned to the party. Because Skip and Amy swear that you showed up there and crawled into his bed and hit on him before throwing up all over the place. You remember waking up there and going back to your apartment the next morning with Skip."

"I do remember that." Despite how much, over the years, she'd wished she could forget that morning. "But I can't recall anything after Mara gave me her drink at that party. I don't think I had more than a few sips of it before everything went fuzzy and then blank. And that drink…" She realized now the implications. "That drink was meant for Mara. Someone was trying to drug Mara."

But had drugged her instead.

"So her murder was premeditated," Kristy said. Her killer had wanted her unable to fight him or her off.

Gretchen shook her head. "No, no, no…"

"Someone had planned to kill Mara that night, or why else drug her?" Who would have done that? Dean, because he thought their flirtation, or more, was going to cost him his career and his marriage?

Or Joey Campbell who knew Mara had caught him stealing those drugs?

Panic quickened Kristy's pulse. Ryder and Trooper Stevens had intended to find Joey, to talk to him. What if he tried shooting at them instead? She needed to warn Ryder. But when she focused on Gretchen again to end their meeting, she noticed the woman was still shaking, still so pale.

She doubted that Gretchen would have killed Mara, but Kristy suddenly realized who else had had a motive. "Amy."

And Gretchen's eyes widened with shock and fear. She shook her head, but that wild look didn't leave her dark eyes. Kristy wasn't the only one feeling scared and panicky right now. "No…"

"She swooped in on Skip pretty quickly after Mara died."

Gretchen shook her head. "It wasn't like that."

"They got married two years after she died, but they must had been seeing each other for a while before then. How long? Right after Mara died?"

And the color rushed back into Gretchen's face now.

"So all Amy needed was Mara out of her way." Kristy leaned forward and studied Gretchen's face more intently. "Did you help her?"

"You're crazy!" Gretchen shouted, and she jumped up from her seat.

But just as quickly as she'd jumped up, she fell as a shot suddenly rang out. People screamed and ran, and Brad rushed forward and tugged Kristy out of her chair to lie flat on the bricks of the outside patio. "We have to get out of here," he said, as he gazed around, trying to see where the shooter was.

His wasn't the only hand grasping Kristy. Gretchen reached out and clutched her hand. "Don't leave me," she murmured weakly.

And Kristy saw the blood pooling beneath the woman, soaking into her clothes.

*Please, God, please don't let her die.*

That bullet in Gretchen had undoubtedly been meant for Kristy. And if the shooter wasn't gone, if he—or she—was still out there somewhere, they might keep firing until they hit her and maybe more innocent people as well.

*Please, God, don't let anyone else get hurt.*

## Chapter Sixteen

Frustration gripped Ryder. Trooper Stevens hadn't been willing to ignore the personal protection order Skip had against Ryder, so he'd refused to let him accompany him to the Holdren estate. And since that was where Joey was working, Ryder wasn't allowed to sit in on his questioning either.

He didn't even know if Trooper Stevens had been able to question them because he'd dropped Ryder off on campus with a promise to check back with him later. He hadn't checked back in yet, but just a couple of hours had passed. So Ryder shouldn't have been feeling as impatient and anxious as he was. But he had this strange sense of foreboding.

While he'd waited to hear back from the trooper, Ryder had seen Dr. Ivan for that cut on his cheek. The doctor had extracted a piece of glass and replaced it with liquid bandage, sealing the wound shut after thoroughly and painfully disinfecting it. Now Ryder was on Sable and riding around the campus.

He should have sought out Kristy and relieved Brad. The young man would be going into overtime soon. But that happened often, with the security department being short-staffed. Ryder should have been protecting Kristy himself, though.

But right now he was protecting himself from what he was beginning to feel for Kristy. Too much...

And if something happened to her...

Pain jabbed his chest at the thought of her being hurt. She'd already been injured when she'd been pushed down the stairs and when her car had gone in the ditch.

And she could have been killed today. There'd been so much glass in her hair. Had she gotten it all out? Had she managed to do that without getting cut? He should have had Trooper Stevens call for an ambulance after all. Should have made sure she was cleaned up without getting wounded.

But even before sustaining the injuries she recently had, she had obviously already been hurting. Just as he had the past ten years, she was blaming herself for Mara's death, feeling as if she'd betrayed her friend. But she hadn't.

No matter how many people believed she had.

He'd been one of those people. And he felt so guilty over it now. Why hadn't he paid more attention to what Joe Campbell had told him the first time they'd talked, just a couple of days after Mara's murder?

*"I think that Kendall girl was drugged..."*

But was the Kendall girl the one the person had

meant to drug? She'd said it had been Mara's drink. Someone had intended to drug his sister.

And kill her?

Had it been premeditated? If so, then Ryder liked Joey Campbell or Dean for the perp. They'd had the most to lose, maybe.

He needed to talk to Dean again. To get him to stop deflecting Ryder's questions and answer them honestly.

But the only one he could trust to be honest with him at St. Michel's was Kristy.

She was too honest and pure to intentionally lie. She just hadn't known what the truth was, and neither did he anymore. He'd been so certain who'd killed his sister, but there had been so much more going on with Mara than he'd realized.

And Kristy had been just as much a victim as his sister had been. Maybe more so, because she hadn't been the intended target like Mara. Kristy had just been collateral damage. And she might be again…if the shooter kept trying for her.

He needed to relieve Brad for certain; he'd never forgive himself if something happened to that poor kid while he was protecting her. He reached inside his coat for his cell just as it began to vibrate with an incoming message.

A transcript from a call to campus security dispatch: *Reports of shots fired at the campus coffeehouse patio. At least one victim down and in need of medical assistance.*

As he read the text, he felt like he'd taken a bullet

to the heart with the sudden sharp pain in his chest. "No!" His shout startled Sable, and the horse reared up. Ryder nearly slipped out of the saddle but grasped with his knees while he clutched the reins. Then he used his knees to nudge the horse into a run as he headed toward that coffeehouse.

Kristy.

It had to be Kristy. He never should have let her out of his sight.

*Please, God, don't let her be hurt. She's already been through too much. Please, God, don't take her away from me, too.*

His eyes stung, and he had to blink furiously to clear his vision. It must have been because of the wind, because he was urging Sable to a great speed across the grass and grounds of the campus. But as fast as the horse ran, they were too late. The ambulance was pulling away, lights flashing, as he drew near. He could have stopped them, but if they were moving that fast, with that much urgency, then the shooting victim was critical.

*Please, God, don't take her. Not yet.*

*Please, no.*

He slowed Sable to a trot as he crossed the parking lot to where troopers were already putting up crime scene tape around the patio of the coffeehouse. And as he drew near, he saw blood pooled on the brick pavers. So much blood.

Kristy's blood?

Thinking about her, worrying about her, must have made him imagine her standing there, talking to a female trooper. But then Kristy saw him and called out, "Ryder!"

He jumped out of the saddle and rushed to her, then pulled her trembling body into his arms. She threw her arms around him and clung tightly to him. "I was so worried about you," she said.

"About me?" he asked. "You're the one who was involved in another shooting. Are you all right?"

Her hair was tangled around her tearstained face and the shoulders of her sweater. He pulled back to scrutinize her and noticed the blood on that sweater; this one was white, and the blood stood out in stark contrast.

"Oh, no, you're wounded! Why weren't you in the ambulance? Why didn't they take you to the hospital?"

She shook her head. "I'm not hurt. This isn't my blood."

"Brad!" he exclaimed. The guy was young, but like Ryder and Dean, he'd already been through boot camp for the Marines. He was in the reserves. He was also already married to his high school sweetheart. Poor Camille…

"No, not Brad—"

"I'm over here, sir," Brad said, and he waved at Ryder from where he was talking to a state police tech in the parking lot. "We're trying to figure out where the shots came from."

"He saved me," Kristy said. "Or maybe Gretchen did. If she hadn't stood up when she had…"

"Gretchen?"

"Gretchen Manchester," she said. "She's friends with Amy Towers-Holdren and Skip. She was there that night."

"Why were you here with her?" he asked. "What did she want?"

"I asked her to meet me," Kristy said. "I wanted the truth. And I got some of it out of her. But at what cost?"

"Is she dead?" Ryder asked. The lights and sirens had been on when the ambulance had pulled away.

"I hope not," Kristy said.

"It didn't look good," the trooper remarked. "Fortunately there was an ambulance in the vicinity. The paramedics acted fast to get her out of here and hopefully into surgery soon. She might have a chance."

"We need to pray for her," Kristy said. "I have to go to the church." And she looked longingly in that direction.

When once Ryder might have argued with her, now he nodded in agreement. He knew Kristy needed to do this, for Gretchen. And Ryder wanted to go with her because he wanted to pray for the woman, too, and for Kristy so that she wouldn't blame herself like he could see she was already doing.

"Do you have everything you need for your report?" he asked the trooper.

The trooper hesitated for a moment. "For now. But both Miss Kendall and that campus security guard think she was the intended target, so she's in danger."

"I know." Ryder's pulse quickened with fear for her safety, for her life.

He never should have let her out of his sight because he'd nearly lost the chance of seeing her again. He needed to thank God for sparing Kristy and pray that He would keep her safe from now on...because Ryder wasn't doing a very good job of it.

The trooper had asked a few more questions before she'd released Kristy to leave with Ryder. He'd helped her onto the horse and rode with her over to the little stone church. While she wasn't comfortable yet on a horse, she was grateful she hadn't had to walk, and she was even more grateful for the warmth and comfort of Ryder's arms around her, of his chest against her back. When they arrived at the church, he dismounted first and reached up to help her down. And when her feet hit the ground, her legs nearly folded beneath her. She was so shaken from what had just happened—from how badly Gretchen had been hurt...

Ryder caught her so that she could lean against him, into him, and draw strength from his strength. He was so strong, had always been so strong, with the way he'd identified and testified against his mother's murderer all those years ago when he'd been just a child.

She laid her head against his chest, where his heart beat strong and fast beneath her ear. And his hands tightened around her waist, and he held on to her as if he didn't intend to let her go.

"I thought it was you," he murmured gruffly, as he lowered his head and settled it against hers. "I was so scared it was you. When I got the report of a shooting and that someone had been hit, I thought it was you."

"It should have been me." Guilt churned in her stomach. "It would have been. If Gretchen hadn't stood up when she did…" That bullet would have hit Kristy. Wouldn't it have? Or would it have gone over her head? Maybe it had been meant as just another warning, but everything had gone so wrong.

"What were you doing with Gretchen Manchester anyway?" Ryder asked. "What did you want to talk to her about?"

"What do you think?" Suddenly so very tired, she released a ragged sigh. But after everything that had happened the past few days, she was entitled to be exhausted. "I was asking her about the thing that consumes us both. Mara's murder. You were right. She didn't leave me at that frat party. I should have never, for a minute, believed that she would…" But Kristy had thought that for nearly ten years, and the guilt churning her stomach intensified so much that she felt nauseous.

"I didn't realize either how wrong that was," Ryder said. "It was Mom who knew her best."

"I knew her better than to think she would have left me there," Kristy said. "Or even get mad at me. In the three years that she and I lived together, we never even had a disagreement…not even over cleanup duty or cooking or…" Tears stung her eyes. "We always worked together. We always stuck together. She wouldn't have left me there…and she didn't. Gretchen admitted to helping Mara carry me back to our apartment."

He tensed and jerked back from her to stare down at her face. "Are you sure you don't have the degree in criminal justice?" he asked. "You're much better at investigating this than I am. Than Trooper Stevens is."

"What did you two learn from Skip and Joey?" she asked.

Ryder shook his head. "I wasn't allowed onto the Holdren estate, and I don't know if Trooper Stevens even got to talk to them. They might have lawyered up or disappeared. I haven't heard from him yet."

"I was so worried that something would happen to you when you were meeting with them." Clearly after the shots fired at his truck, he was as much a target as she was.

"And you were the one who was shot at again," he said, and his long body shuddered. Then he reached for her, cupped her face in his hands and slowly leaned down and brushed his mouth across hers.

Kristy kissed him back, her lips savoring the softness of his. The sweetness of the kiss... But there was attraction too. And so much regret...

This wasn't the time and place. She doubted there would ever be a time and place for them. She stepped back and reminded him, "I really want to pray for Gretchen."

He nodded. "I do, too." He took her hand in his, and they walked up the steps and into the stone structure together.

The last time she'd been in here, just a few hours

ago, Kristy hadn't been comforted. She'd been on edge, worrying about Ryder. Maybe that was why she felt better now, with her hand in Ryder's. Or maybe he was giving her more comfort than the church.

It was aglow with light from the sconces, and that light reflected in the stained glass windows, bouncing myriad colors around the interior. She and Ryder chose a row and sat down, and together they prayed for the woman who might become the next victim of Mara's murderer.

"Please, God," Kristy implored Him, "let Gretchen survive. She's young with so much life ahead of her, like Mara…"

But Mara was gone, and none of it made any sense to Kristy. The more she learned about that night, the more confused she became.

"Please, God," Ryder spoke aloud as he clasped Kristy's hand yet in his. "Please, help us figure out who killed Mara so that we can stop him—"

"Or her," Kristy interjected.

"From killing again," Ryder finished. "And help Gretchen survive her injury and recover fully."

"Yes, please," Kristy fervently added. She wanted to pray for more, but those prayers would have been selfish, prayers about herself and Ryder and how she was beginning to fall for him. She wanted to go on holding his hand forever, sitting at his side, like they were.

She had no idea how long they'd been inside the church. It had already been late afternoon when they'd walked in, so the lights had been on and burning low. But suddenly they burned out, plunging them into darkness.

Outside the church, night had fallen already. No light filtered through the stained glass windows, just the sound of the horse's faint whinny, as if it was startled. Or scared.

Was the shooter out there? Would he or she come into the church to finish what they'd tried at the coffeehouse?

To kill Kristy?

## Chapter Seventeen

Ryder wasn't sure what had happened the night before in the church. And it wasn't just the lights going
off that had unsettled him. It was sitting there, holding hands with Kristy, praying together...

But they'd done more than pray and hold hands.

He'd kissed her.

And he hadn't even apologized. He should have.
Kissing her had been ill-timed and ill-advised, but he
hadn't been able to help himself. So many emotions
had been reeling through him.

Relief. He'd been relieved that she wasn't the one
who'd been shot. And he'd felt a little guilty about
that relief. About poor Gretchen...

Even though she'd obviously been lying about
the past, she hadn't deserved to get shot. When he'd
called Trooper Stevens to check in with him after he'd
gotten Kristy safely out of the dark church and back
to her apartment, the young lawman had reported

that Gretchen had survived surgery. So maybe his and Kristy's prayers for her had worked.

She was still critical though, so she needed more prayers. Prayers to regain consciousness, so she could repeat what she'd told Kristy to the trooper. He hadn't had a chance to talk to Skip or Joey. Joey was MIA, and Skip had claimed he'd already answered enough questions. He wasn't going to talk to anyone else unless he was subpoenaed to do so, and then he would have a lawyer present with him.

That gave Ryder a little flash of hope that maybe he hadn't been wrong about him all these years. He'd only been wrong about Kristy. She hadn't knowingly been lying for the guy. She'd been lied to.

Mara hadn't left her at the frat house, so how had she gotten back there? She had to have been the woman that Tyler Milanowski had seen being carried that night. And wouldn't it have had to have been Skip?

Unless someone had just dumped her back at the party to skew the timeline of when Mara had been murdered.

Or…

Ryder had spent the night tossing and turning, trying to figure it all out. And trying to forget about that kiss.

About the silkiness of Kristy's lips, the sweetness of her breath…

He gave up on trying to sleep just around dawn, which was good because he was already up when someone started pounding on the door. He rushed to it and pulled it open with one hand on his holster, prepared for anything.

He expected to find Kristy, afraid because of something that happened. Instead he found Dean on his doorstep. The guy shoved him back, stepped inside and closed the door behind him. "You going to use that gun on me?" Dean asked.

"That depends," Ryder said, even as he pulled his hand away from his holster.

"On what?" Dean asked. "I didn't kill your sister. I wouldn't have ever done anything to hurt her." His throat moved as if he was struggling to swallow, then he added, "Or you."

Ryder wanted to believe him, wanted to have the faith to trust his friend like he used to, but so much had happened. He, and especially Kristy, had been in danger so many times. "I didn't know she had that crush on you."

"I did," Dean said. "And I didn't do anything to discourage it. I should have, but I was flattered. I let my ego get the best of me, let it lead me to make bad decisions—"

Ryder gasped and nearly reached, not for his gun but for Dean's face, with his fist as fury coursed through him. "You took advantage of my sister!"

"No!" Dean protested. "No, but I didn't shut her down and make it clear to her that I didn't have feelings like that for her."

Ryder narrowed his eyes with skepticism. "Really?"

"Mara was a beautiful girl. A smart, vivacious

girl that everyone on campus was enthralled with, and the fact that she was enthralled with me…" Dean sighed and pushed a hand through his hair. "I was an idiot. And it wasn't just Mara I let flatter me with the flirting. I let Amy Towers and Gretchen Manchester flirt with me, too, like it was some kind of competition and I was the prize. I know better now. I know I was no prize."

Ryder snorted and nodded in agreement. Dean was definitely not the man Ryder had thought he was—a man he could trust.

"After Mara died and you were so devastated and so was Kristy, I realized I was walking a fine line that I never should have even let myself get near. And after that, I vowed to do better. I vowed to *be* better."

This was something Ryder hadn't asked him yet because he hadn't wanted to pry, but he asked now, "Why did your wife divorce you then, if you're truly a better man?"

"Because I still wasn't the man she wanted," he said. "She left me for someone else. Someone who loves her so much that he wants to make her feel special instead of feeling special himself. He's good to the kids, too. And he's made me realize how selfish and self-centered I've been, how I haven't been a good husband or father or friend…and I can't change the past, but I'm trying to do better."

"That's all anyone can do," Ryder agreed.

"You can't change the past either," Dean said. "You can't bring Mara back."

"I know," he said. "That's not what I'm trying to

do. I'm just trying to get her the justice she's been denied so long."

"Are you trying to get it for her or for you?" Dean asked.

And Ryder chuckled. "Maybe I'm a selfish, self-centered man, too. Maybe I do want it for me."

"There's nothing wrong with that," Dean said. "Especially not if you're able to move on after you get it."

"And if no one gets hurt," Ryder said. But it was already too late for that. Gretchen Manchester had been shot. And Kristy had been hurt, too, when she'd been pushed down the stairs. She could have gotten shot as well. There had been so many attempts. He had to make certain there were no more.

He couldn't lose her…but she wasn't even his to lose.

Kristy couldn't lose Ryder. He'd stuck with her all day, trailing her from the apartment to the lecture hall. But she'd barely been able to focus on teaching; she was too worried about Gretchen.

"I want to go see her," she told him after her last class. "And I want to pick up the loaner car from the body shop that's going to fix my car. You and I can't ride Sable everywhere."

Ryder sighed but nodded. "You're right. My truck is at the body shop, too, getting the rear window replaced, but I can borrow a campus vehicle and drive you into town."

"You could have Brad bring me," she said. "You don't need to watch over me every second. I know you're busy."

And spending so much time with him was making it impossible for her to forget about that kiss and her attraction to him. An attraction that had no hope of ever being anything more. All they had in common was Mara, and she was gone.

Kristy wanted to make sure that Gretchen wasn't as well. She'd survived the surgery, but she was still in critical condition. Kristy might not be allowed to see her, but she needed to go down to the hospital, bring some flowers, say some prayers in the hospital chapel...

She'd been doing so much praying lately. So something good needed to happen. Gretchen needed to recover.

"My main priority is making sure nothing happens to you," he said with such intensity that she shivered.

But then the look in his blue eyes had warmth flooding her heart. She could fall for him so deeply... if she trusted that they had a future together once they'd caught the killer and if she believed he could forgive her if she'd been wrong about Skip.

She'd been so certain that she'd been his alibi—that things had happened the way she'd been told. But now she had no idea what had really happened or even whom to believe.

Ryder reached for her face, then cupped her cheek in his palm. "Kristy..." His gaze slipped to her lips, and he looked like he wanted to kiss her again. But just as he began to lower his head, his cell rang. He pulled his hand from her face to grab his phone out of his pocket. "It's Trooper Stevens," he said.

Her pulse quickened. Was Gretchen awake? Or…
*Please, God, let her be okay.*

"You'll let me sit in on the interview?" he asked.
"Yes, I'll be there." He clicked off his cell. "I guess I
will have Brad drive you to get that rental."

"What?" she asked. "Did Skip agree to talk to the
trooper? Or Joey?"

He shook his head. "No, the trooper found Tyler
Milanowski. He brought him to the local police post
in Eagle Valley for questioning. Maybe I should bring
you with me there, so he can determine whether or not
you were the woman he saw being carried."

"That was a long time ago," she said.

"You still look the same."

"Everybody keeps telling me I haven't changed."

"You don't sound happy about that," he said.

"I don't want to stay the same," she said. "I want
to be stronger, wiser, happier…"

He smiled. "I think you already are stronger and
wiser."

And maybe once Mara's murder was solved, they
could both be happier. "I have some old pictures of
me and Mara on my phone," she said. "I can forward
them to you."

"I already have some," he said. "And you're right.
He should see a picture of Mara, too."

*Mara…*

She was his focus, rightfully so, as she was Kristy's
too. Mara…and Gretchen. Less than an hour later,
she carried a bouquet of daisies into Eagle Valley's
only hospital. It was small, so small there was only

one waiting room, and when she walked into it, she saw Amy. But Amy must have seen her first because she was already charging toward her. She jerked the vase of flowers from Kristy's grasp and smashed it onto the floor.

"Get out of here! Get out of here! You have no right to be here!"

The violence of her reaction startled Kristy, and she regretted telling Brad to wait for her in the parking garage. He'd parked the campus vehicle he'd used to drive her to town next to the loaner from the body shop. But she'd thought she would be safe in the hospital. That nobody would try anything here.

"What's wrong with you?" she asked Amy. "Are you the one who shot at me, and you're furious that you hit Gretchen instead?"

Amy pulled back her arm and swung her hand toward Kristy's face. But Kristy caught her wrist in her grasp and held it tightly when Amy tried to wrest it free. "If you hit me, I will press charges."

"How—how dare you accuse me of hurting my best friend? I'm not like you. I wouldn't hurt Gretchen like you hurt Mara."

Kristy shook her head. "We both know now that never happened. Mara and Gretchen carried me home that night. I never threw myself at Skip."

"Then how did you wind up in his bed?" Amy asked.

"If Mara and Gretchen had to carry me back to my apartment, how would I have been able to get myself to Skip's?"

"I don't know that you're telling the truth," Amy said. "Gretchen never told me that."

Kristy chuckled. "I doubt that. If you're really best friends, she would have told you. You would have known the truth. And I can't help but wonder why you'd lie all those years ago."

"You have no proof that any of that happened," Amy said, and she tugged free of Kristy. But instead of swinging again, she wrapped her arms around herself. "They don't know if Gretchen is even going to make it."

"I've been praying that she does," Kristy said. "And I'll keep praying. And as for the truth, Ryder and Trooper Stevens are interviewing a man right now who may shed some light on that."

"Who? What are you talking about?" Amy asked, her voice sharp with nerves.

"There was a witness—someone who saw a man carrying a woman on campus the very night Mara died."

"There were a lot of parties that night," Amy said. "It could have been anyone."

"Ryder has pictures with him. He'll figure it out." Kristy stepped a little closer to Amy and warned her, "He'll figure out who killed Mara and who shot Gretchen, too."

Amy trembled again and tightened her arms around herself. "None of that has anything to do with me."

"I think it does," Kristy replied. "You wouldn't have had Gretchen lie all these years if you weren't hiding something." But was she hiding her guilt or her husband's?

Knowing that she wasn't going to get to see Gretchen and that Brad was waiting for her in the parking garage, Kristy left her broken vase of flowers on the floor for Amy to clean up and turned and walked away. A quick trip in the elevator brought her to the parking level. As she stepped out of the open doors, she had a strange feeling that someone was out there, waiting for her.

Had Amy taken the stairs and beaten her down here?

Or was someone else out here?

Like the shooter...

Brad was supposed to be here; he'd walked her to the elevator when they'd arrived at the hospital. And he'd been careful to park his campus security truck where he could see the elevator and wait for her return.

But she doubted she would have felt this uneasy if Brad was the one she felt watching her.

When she looked at the campus security vehicle, she didn't see anyone sitting inside it. Where was Brad?

Her pulse quickened with fear...for herself and for him.

Where was he?

Was he okay?

She heard footsteps on the concrete, coming from somewhere behind her, but she was too afraid to wait and see if it was him. So she clicked the key fob for her loaner. There was also an alarm button, and she clicked that as well, making the lights flash and the horn blow.

And she hoped that scared away whoever was out there, because she had a feeling that *whoever was out there* wanted to do more than scare her.

# Chapter Eighteen

In his role as head of campus security, Ryder had done quite a few interviews, and he'd never had a problem getting witnesses to reveal all they knew and for suspects to crack. Even as an MP, he'd had a good reputation for getting the most information out of whomever he spoke to. The only person he'd found it difficult to question had been Kristy, but he realized now that was because she truly hadn't been able to remember.

This guy, who sat in a windowless interrogation room at the state police post, was just pretending he couldn't remember. Ryder could tell the difference; he wasn't so sure that the young trooper could. Stevens had put restrictions on Ryder sitting in on the interrogation. He could listen, but if he wanted to interject, he had to run it past Stevens first.

"Can I show him some photos?" Ryder asked. "See if they jog his memory?"

"Nothing to jog, man," Tyler Milanowski replied.

"College was a long time ago. With all the parties and crap, I don't remember much from that time."

"You don't remember much from the other day either," the trooper pointed out, "when you agreed to meet with Mr. Lewis here."

"Hey, I heard gunshots and got out of there," the man said, and his face grew pale. His throat moved as he swallowed hard.

The guy was probably Kristy's age, but he looked older, with thinning hair and hollow-looking eyes. Ryder doubted that his partying had stopped after his college days. So how had he afforded to buy such a nice place? The trooper had tracked the guy down at his place of work, and it was a part-time job at one of Skip's dad's businesses.

"I didn't know what this guy wanted to see me about, and when I heard the shooting, I got scared," Tyler continued.

And that was probably the only truthful thing he'd said since Ryder had joined the interrogation. Tyler looked scared even now as he fidgeted in his chair and clasped his slightly shaking hands together.

"You have every reason to be scared," Ryder said. "The person who shot at my vehicle at your condo complex shot another woman later that day. She may not make it."

"Are—are you sure it was the same shooter?" Tyler asked.

And Ryder knew that Tyler knew who that shooter was. Trooper Stevens glanced at Ryder and nodded slightly, and Ryder knew that he knew, too, and that he was willing to step back and let Ryder take over this interview.

"Ballistics confirmed it," Ryder said vaguely. According to Stevens, it had confirmed the same caliber of weapon, but there hadn't been time yet for the results to come back confirming it was the exact same weapon. But Ryder was sure it was the same—as sure as he was that he'd always been right.

"I guess you were lucky you got out of there when you did," Ryder said. "You could have been shot like that woman was…because she knew the truth." Kristy had been so convinced that the shooter meant to hit her and that Gretchen had been hit instead. But what if Gretchen's meeting with Kristy—talking to her—had scared the killer so much that he'd had to silence her?

"Truth about what?" Tyler asked.

"Truth about what happened to my sister ten years ago," he said. "This is the picture I wanted to show you." Instead of pulling up one of the photos he'd copied of his sister and Kristy where they'd been smiling and laughing, he pulled up one of just his sister from the crime scene. Joe Campbell had taken photos before the state police had taken over the case, and Ryder had taken a picture of one of them when Joe had shared his records with them the other day.

The guy's throat moved as if he was struggling to swallow. Then he finally rasped out. "I don't know anything about that."

"But you saw something that night," he said. "Something you reported to campus security before this murder was discovered."

"That wasn't the woman who was being carried."

"So you do remember," the trooper remarked.

"I-It was a long time ago," Tyler maintained. "I—I can't be sure of anything."

From Joe's notes about the report, that had probably been the case at the time—when he'd called campus security that night. But later…

"When was it?" Ryder asked. "Was it at the memorial for my sister? Was that when you saw that man and woman again? Was that when you started piecing it together?"

The guy's face flushed, and he shook his head. "I—I didn't piece anything together. I don't know anything."

"You know enough to get paid well for barely working for Skip Holdren," Ryder said. "And your condo, in a Holdren development, is completely paid off." Stevens had checked into all of that before bringing the man in for questioning.

"Yeah, I got a good job," Tyler said. "I'm smart with my money."

"Eventually people get sick of paying," Ryder remarked. "That's probably what happened to Gretchen Manchester, why she was shot and might die. Eventually it's easier to kill a witness than to keep paying them off. And since that person already killed once, what's one or two or three more murders?"

The guy's throat moved again, and he choked and sputtered, "I don't know what you're talking about."

"The truth," Ryder said. "It's time you told it. I'm going to show you one more photo."

The guy flinched and closed his eyes. "Not that murdered girl…"

"No, this girl," he said. And he pulled up the photo of Kristy. Mara was with her, but she was very much alive. They had their arms around each other, and they were laughing so hard that their faces were flushed and their eyes sparkling. Mara had texted the picture to him just a week before she died.

The guy sighed. "Yeah, the dark haired one. That was her."

"And the guy?"

"He's not in this picture," Tyler replied.

"No, but you know who he is. You've been blackmailing him for years."

"Hey—"

"Unless you want to wind up in the hospital like Gretchen, you'd be smart to start telling the truth right now. The whole truth."

"We can talk to a prosecutor about the blackmailing," the trooper chimed in. "Get you immunity for that. I'm not so sure about the accessory to murder charge you're looking at though…"

Ryder suppressed the smile that tugged at his lips. Stevens was young, but he was good.

"Accessory to murder?" Tyler asked. "I had nothing to do with that." And he pointed at Ryder's phone. He was obviously referring to the first photo he'd been shown on it, from the murder scene. "I didn't even know that happened when I called campus security that night. I just wanted to make sure that girl was okay. And I had no idea who the guy carrying her was…"

"Until later," Ryder said.

The guy sighed and nodded. "Until later."

"And then you made the most of it," Ryder remarked. "You've been playing a dangerous game, Milanowski, and I'm surprised you're still alive."

"I got insurance," Tyler said. "I told some people what I know, and I made sure Holdren knows that if he came after me, people would tell the police that it was him."

*It was him.*

"That was smart," Ryder said. "It was also obstruction of justice." For nearly ten years, Skip Holdren had been a free man while Mara had been dead. Fury coursed through Ryder, and now he was the one whose hands were shaking.

He wanted the justice Mara had been denied so long, and he wanted to take it into his own hands.

Kristy needed to settle her madly pounding heart, and so she wanted to go where she always went for peace. To the church…

"I'm sorry," Brad said—again—as they walked from the parking lot, down the brick pathway to the church. Shadows were already gathering as the sun slipped low in the sky. "I didn't mean to scare you like that back at the parking garage."

His had been the footsteps she'd heard, the ones following her. He'd been worried about her and had gone up to the waiting room just in time to witness her scene with Amy. In the heat of her argument, she hadn't noticed him, or when he'd tried to wave her down at the elevator. So he'd had to run down the stairs to catch up with her in the parking garage.

"I'm just relieved you're all right," she said. "I was so worried when I didn't see you in your truck." And she wasn't sure she would have been able to forgive herself if someone else had gotten hurt because of her, like Gretchen. She hadn't been able to pray for her in the hospital chapel, so she wanted to pray for her again here, at the campus church.

"I was so worried when I saw Mrs. Holdren going at you like that in the waiting room," he said. "But you really held your own, Miss Kendall. You didn't need me to protect you from her."

She'd once needed Mara to protect her from the mean girls. But now that Mara was gone, she'd had to learn how to defend herself. Maybe if she'd known how back then, she would have been able to protect Mara, too. Or at least she would have figured out what happened sooner. Hopefully Ryder was putting all of the events of that night together now, with Trooper Stevens, and this would all be over soon.

But what would that mean? Would Ryder leave once he had justice for his sister? Would he return to the rodeo or his family ranch?

Kristy wanted to stay here, despite all the bad things that had happened at St. Michel's. There had been good things, too.

*Mara...*

Kristy had only known her three years, but Mara would be with her forever—in her heart and in her faith and in the strength she'd given her.

"Thank you," she said to Brad. And she reached out and squeezed his arm as they walked up the steps and into the church. "I appreciate you looking out for me. I hate that it's put you in danger, too."

"I'm fine, Miss Kendall. Ryder's training is really good. Can't believe he was a rodeo rider and not always in law enforcement. He's taught me more than I learned at the police academy. I know he's just here because of his sister, but I sure hope he stays at St. Michel's after he finds the killer."

She hoped so as well, but that wasn't her decision to make. And she was sure she wouldn't factor into it at all. Ryder's only interest in her had been in helping him get the justice he'd been seeking for so long. That kiss…

She wasn't sure what that kiss had been except that she thought of it far too often just as she did Ryder. While she hadn't been in danger at the hospital or in the parking garage, she worried that he was…especially if he was closing in on the killer.

So when she slid down a row and took a seat to pray, she didn't pray just for Gretchen. She prayed for Ryder, too. She prayed that he stayed safe while he sought justice.

She prayed so long that the last light outside slipped away, leaving the stained glass windows dark and the only illumination from the sconces on the walls. But then they went dark, too.

Brad groaned.

And Kristy chuckled. "It must be the breaker again. It keeps going out." That was all it had been the last few times it had happened in the church. "We can leave now."

Brad chuckled, too. "I can tell that you'd like to stay. I'll just go throw the breaker. Pastor Howard showed me where it is when this happened during the rehearsal for my wedding. My wife and I got married in this church."

"That must have been beautiful." She could imagine how it would look with flowers everywhere and twinkling lights and a runner on the stone floor that the bride would follow down to the front of the church, her groom and Pastor Howard.

And in this vision in her head, she saw that groom wearing a black cowboy hat with his tuxedo. And outside the church, Sable, with flowers woven into her mane, would wait for the couple. "Beautiful..." she murmured.

She'd always had a big imagination; it was why she'd wanted to be a writer. But that was probably the most fantastical thing she could have imagined. Marrying Ryder.

"It was beautiful once the lights came back on," Brad said. "I'll be right back, Miss Kendall." His footsteps echoed throughout the church as he walked down the aisle toward the back and the stairs that led to the basement. Only a short time passed before the sound of footsteps echoed again as someone walked back up the aisle, toward her.

But the lights hadn't come back on.

And even though she couldn't see anything, she knew who had joined her. She knew because a chill of foreboding and fear passed through her, making her shiver.

"I figured I'd find you here."

"Hello, Skip," she said, and now she prayed for herself.

And for Brad.

Because if the lights didn't come on soon, if he didn't come back, something must have happened to him. Skip must have hurt him somehow...like he intended to hurt her now.

# Chapter Nineteen

When Trooper Stevens headed to the Holdren estate to arrest Skip, Ryder headed back to St. Michel's. Stevens had told Ryder that he was welcome to wait for him to return to the state police post with the suspect. The local district attorney was already waiting there so she could question Holdren herself since she knew he wanted his attorney present. But Ryder knew Skip wasn't home.

He knew because Brad didn't answer his cell.

Brad was a good guard. He always answered his cell. No matter what time it was, even if it was the middle of the night and the guy was in a sound sleep, he answered his cell. The only reason he wasn't answering now was because he couldn't.

Ryder's pulse raced with fear…for his employee and for the woman Brad was supposed to be protecting: Kristy.

*Please, God, let them both be all right.*

Since getting to know Kristy, Ryder had prayed

more than he ever had in his entire life, and his step-mom was a religious woman. But after Mara's death, he'd faltered in his faith because he'd felt like God had failed the people he'd loved the most. First his mother and then Mara.

Now he was afraid He might fail Kristy and Brad. Even if Brad hadn't sent him a text earlier to let Ryder know where they'd gone after the hospital, he would have known. And when he walked up to the church, he wasn't surprised to find it dark inside either.

And he would bet the breaker hadn't accidentally tripped this time; someone had purposely tripped it to plunge the church in darkness. And probably to get Brad out of his way.

Ryder was careful when he walked up the steps, keeping his boots from hitting the stones loud enough to make noise. And when he pushed open the door, he did it only wide enough for him to slip inside, and as he did, he nearly tripped over something lying on the ground.

Brad.

He dropped to his knees and felt around until he found Brad's wrist. A pulse beat strong and steady, so he was alive. But how badly was he hurt that he was unmoving and unconscious? Ryder needed to call for an ambulance and for police backup.

But a soft voice drifted back to him from the front of the church, and he tensed with fear for her. He didn't have time to wait for help to arrive.

"I had a feeling that you would show up, Skip,"

she said, "after I talked to Amy at the hospital. Is she upset that you shot Gretchen?"

"She thinks I was trying to hit you," he replied.

"But that wasn't the case—that time," Kristy said. "You were worried she was going to tell me too much, that she was going to reveal enough that I could figure out what really happened..."

"That night you were at the house," he said. "I told them both to stay away from you. But Gretchen..." He sighed. "She didn't think it was a big deal that you were back. She thought there was no way you could figure anything out about that night..."

"When you tried to drug Mara but I got the drug instead..." she murmured with a little hitch in her voice as if she was trying not to cry. "Were you intending to kill her then? Had you planned it?"

Skip let out a bitter chuckle. "You're so naive, Kristy, even now all these years later. I didn't want to kill Mara. I loved her, and I wanted what she kept denying me—telling me she wasn't ready...that she didn't feel that way about me..."

Ryder's hands curled into fists as that fury coursed through him again. He wanted to hurt Skip. Badly... but he had to be careful because he knew Skip had a gun, and he probably had the barrel pressed up against Kristy's head or her heart right now.

If Ryder moved too quickly, Skip could pull that trigger. He would kill her before Ryder could even get close to them. He could kill her right in front of Ryder, just like that carjacker had killed his mother.

But it was so dark in the church, Ryder couldn't see anything. Even as his eyes began to adjust to the shadows, he could only see what was closest to him. Brad.

His head was bleeding onto the stone floor. He was badly injured. He needed help. But if Ryder called for help and Skip heard sirens, he would probably kill Kristy quickly and try to get away. Like he'd gotten away with one murder for nearly ten years.

"She didn't love you, Skip," Kristy said softly, as if she didn't want to hurt his feelings. And maybe she didn't. No matter what kind of person he was, Kristy was a good one. One of the best.

"Why not?" Skip asked, and he sounded like he really wanted to know. "You knew her so well. What was it? Why didn't she love me? Was it because of Dean Stolz? Was she seeing him?"

"He was married then," Kristy said. "While Mara flirted with him, that was a line she never would have crossed. She was a good girl, Skip. And she was a really wonderful friend. I should have figured out sooner that she wouldn't have left me at the frat house that night, especially with the condition I was in."

"That was what Gretchen told you," he said as if confirming his suspicion. "I couldn't get close enough to hear, not with that campus cop sticking so close to you. But I knew she was running her mouth."

"She's not the only one who's talking now," Kristy said. "I think Amy will—"

"Amy will protect me and especially the Holdren name," he said. "She always has. She was even more worried about you coming back than I was. She was the one who messed with your stuff and wrote on your mirror. She even followed you here a couple of times, trying to scare you off like she tried to scare Mara away from me." It sounded like he was grinning as he bragged. "I have a good life with her and our kids. I've been happy, Kristy. Why did you have to come back?" He snorted. "I know why—that campus cowboy cop."

Ryder had never minded being called that until now, when Skip said it.

"This is all his fault," Skip said. "If he would have just let it go…"

"You killed his sister, Skip," Kristy said. "He can't let that go. He can't let Mara go, and neither can I. We miss her so much."

The pain in Kristy's voice echoed the pain that had been in Ryder's heart these past nearly ten years. The hollow ache of loss.

"You loved her, too," Kristy continued. "How can you live with yourself? How can you have been happy all these years after what you did to her?"

Because he had no conscience. Because he was a sociopath. And knowing that, Ryder also knew that Skip would have no problem taking Kristy's life, too, just like he had Mara's. Ryder had to get closer. So he slipped off his boots and then he started, in just his socks, down the aisle toward where he knew Kristy usually sat.

And he hoped he could get to her, that he could get her away from Skip or at least get between them. He couldn't lose Kristy.

\* \* \*

Kristy knew Ryder was in the church. She'd heard the soft creak of the door when he'd slipped inside; fortunately Skip hadn't heard it, or at least he hadn't reacted, but she'd kept talking to distract him. The person who'd come into the church had been so quiet and so careful, she'd known it wasn't Pastor Howard. Hopefully the older man would stay away, so he didn't get hurt.

Like Brad.

Poor Brad had to be hurt, or he would have switched the breaker to turn on the lights again. He would have come back.

But he'd been gone a long time.

*Please, God, make sure that he's okay, that he isn't dead. Please, God, help him. Help us.*

Skip might have been sending her warnings before, but she knew that he intended to kill her now. And if he knew Ryder was in the church, he would try to kill him, too. She had to keep talking, had to distract Skip, and maybe somehow she could reach him. If he had a conscience.

"I know you loved Mara," she told him again.

"Everyone loved Mara…" he remarked with awe in his voice. "I'd never met anyone like her."

"Me neither," Kristy agreed. "She lit up a room. She lit up my life. She was everything good in the world—so much love and happiness and fun."

Skip chuckled as if remembering something about his former girlfriend. "She really was. She could make studying fun."

"She always did." Despite the danger, Kristy smiled. "I often think about what she'd be doing now, if she hadn't died…about how many kids she would have had, because family had been everything to her. She loved her mom and dad so much. And especially her brother."

She felt the shift in the air, the sudden tension, and knew Ryder was closer—close enough that she'd been physically able to feel his reaction to her words. "That's why he's so determined to get justice for her murder."

Skip snorted. "He doesn't want justice. He wants revenge. He's going to kill me," he said, his voice quavering slightly with fear.

He had no compunction about taking another life like Mara's and maybe Gretchen's and Brad's, but he was scared to lose his own. She couldn't necessarily blame him; she was scared now, too.

But she wasn't scared just for herself.

"He won't do that," Kristy said. "He's a really good man. He knows you have a wife and kids who love you—"

Skip snorted again. "Amy loves the Holdren name and money. That's what matters most to her. She's like my dad that way. He kept paying to make sure people wouldn't talk. He was going to offer you money, too, but I stopped him. I knew you didn't remember, but if he offered you money, then you'd figure out what really happened that night."

"You put something in Mara's drink," she said. "But she gave it to me."

"I didn't realize that at the party," Skip said. "I didn't see you and Mara and Gretchen leave. I thought she was the one who was passed out. So I waited a bit, waited for Gretchen to leave, and I snuck in—"

"To our apartment."

"I had a key," he said. "I took Mara's once and copied them."

He had been really obsessed with her, just like Ryder had suspected when he'd read those texts and letters. He'd been right all along about Skip, and she'd foolishly kept defending the man, defending a killer. Sick with that realization, her stomach churned.

"I remember that," Kristy said. "She thought she left them in the stables."

"That's where I left them after I copied them, so she would find them there," he said. "Joey saw me stash them there, and after the murder, he started asking for money. Just like Tyler Milanowski. I should have killed them instead. I should have killed them all."

"You shouldn't have killed anyone," Kristy said. "Life is too precious to take."

Skip chuckled. "You're so sweet, Kristy. You're the only one I really didn't want to hurt."

"You wanted to hurt Mara?" she asked, appalled.

"I wanted Mara," he said. "But she wasn't drugged. She wasn't drunk. So she figured it out quick when I walked into your apartment. She realized I'd drugged her drink and copied her keys. And she was going to call the campus cops. I had to stop her. We fought…" He shuddered next to her and it shook her seat. "She fought so hard. She grabbed the knife from the drawer and came at me. It was really self-defense."

Or at least that was what he must have told himself all these years. It was what he must have told his dad and everybody else who'd helped him cover up his crime. She hated to think that anyone would have knowingly helped a murderer escape justice.

She hated that she had, but at least she hadn't known the truth. Did Ryder understand though? Did he really forgive her when he'd been right all these years?

"Then you should have told the truth back then, Skip," she said. "You should have called to get her medical attention. But you let her die…"

"No, no, she was dead," he said, his voice cracking with emotion. "There was so much blood, so much of it…"

"You still should have called for help," she insisted. "But instead you grabbed me and carried me back to your frat house. You used me for an alibi."

He sighed. "It worked. All these years it worked. But then *he* had to bring you back here. That crazy cowboy."

That crazy cowboy was close. She could feel him in the quickening of her pulse, in the racing of her heart. She had already been afraid, but now she was even more so. Because she knew he was going to make his move. He had to…for her sake. And for Brad's.

Unless it was already too late for Brad.

When the lights had gone off and she'd heard someone coming, she'd called campus security. But she'd muted her cell and dropped it into her purse so Skip wouldn't know. But help had to be coming.

Was that how Ryder had found them?

Or had he just somehow known this was where she would be?

"He won't kill you," she said. "He believes in God, in prayer, in the good in people…in the good in himself."

Skip snorted again. "Kristy, you're still so naive. So trusting. I don't want to do this to you. I don't want to hurt you."

But she knew he was turning that gun on her. And she finally moved—lunging backward, onto the floor—and as she did, she felt someone pass her.

And then gunshots shattered the peace of the quiet, dark little stone church.

# *Chapter Twenty*

Ryder could have killed Skip. He could have done it and called it what Skip had tried calling Mara's murder: self-defense. Skip had been armed with his own gun, with the one he'd kept firing at Kristy and Ryder over the past few days. So if Ryder had fired his gun back at Skip, he could have called it self-defense, but that still wouldn't have made it right. Not when he knew he could take Skip down without killing him.

Ryder would have known the truth. And Kristy would have, too. And then she would have thought she was wrong about another man, like she'd been wrong about Skip when she'd provided him that alibi.

When she'd believed his lies and the lies of his accomplices.

So Ryder hadn't pulled his trigger. He hadn't fired his weapon. It was Skip who sprayed bullets around the little stone church. He'd fired so many times before Ryder had wrested the gun from his grasp and knocked him out with a solid punch to his jaw. Even though his knuckles stung now, and he shook his hand to ease the pain, the punch had been satisfying.

He'd struck Skip so hard in his weak jaw that he'd knocked him out for a little while. But Skip was awake now, sitting in the back seat of Trooper Stevens' state police SUV, while Stevens sat in the front, turned around to take his statement.

Brad, fortunately, was awake, too. An ambulance had taken him away moments ago to the hospital. He needed a CT scan and some stitches, but hopefully he would be okay. That was probably due to Kristy's prayers.

She'd been saying them when the gun had gone off. She'd been praying for all of them. Even Skip.

Maybe that was why Ryder hadn't pulled his trigger. Why he hadn't taken the cowboy justice he'd intended to take—revenge—just like Skip had suspected. But since getting to know Kristy, he wanted to be the better man that she thought he was.

Trooper Stevens stepped out of the front seat of his car and walked slowly over to where Ryder sat on the stone steps of the church. Kristy was inside with Pastor Howard. Ryder hadn't even talked to her since Skip had fired his gun.

The second Ryder had wrested the gun from him, the lights had flashed on and troopers had stormed inside, brandishing their weapons. He knew she was all right only because he'd heard her tell Trooper Stevens that.

From the grim look on Stevens' face, he had something to tell Ryder that he didn't think the head of security was going to like. "He's denying it all," Stevens said. "Says you set him up. That you planted that gun on him. That you're trying to frame him for your sister's murder."

Ryder laughed.

And the trooper's eyes widened with shock. "I thought you'd be furious. And with the high-priced lawyer he's got, he might get away with it, Ryder."

"There's no chance of that, thanks to Kristy Kendall." The woman Skip had once used to escape justice had ensured that he would not escape it again.

Ryder pulled his cell from his pocket and showed Stevens the transcript of the call Kristy had placed to campus security. "There's a recording of it, too. Skip's full confession to everything. He even said enough to bring down his dad as an accessory after the fact."

Stevens whistled and grinned. "This is going to be fun."

It wasn't fun for Ryder. It was just over. Finally. He watched as Stevens returned to his vehicle, climbed inside and drove away with the lights flashing. He wasn't taking Skip in just for questioning anymore. The man would be arrested, and with the admission of how his father had bought his freedom all these years, there was no way he would even be granted bail. He'd be held until his trial unless he was smart and took a deal.

Dean walked out of the church and dropped onto the steps next to Ryder. "Well, cowboy, you got your justice," he said. "You were right. All these years you were certain that it was Skip Holdren. You weren't wrong."

"Not about Skip…"

"About me?" Dean asked. "I'm sorry, Ryder. I'm sorry I'm not as good a man as you are."

"I'm not as good a man as I want to be either," Ryder said. Because he'd once wanted to pull that trigger. He'd once wanted to take his own justice. And that would have made him little better than Skip.

And he wanted to be better.

For Kristy.

"So are you going to leave now?" Dean asked. "Go back to the rodeo?"

Ryder shook his head. "I'm too old for the rodeo."

"Your ranch?"

"I should go home," he said. He needed to talk to his mom and dad, tell them what had happened and maybe he could get his father to look at him again. To forgive him.

Because Ryder had finally forgiven himself.

It wasn't his fault his mother had died. He'd only been six at the time. He couldn't have saved her. But he'd made certain she'd gotten justice. And the same thing with Mara. He couldn't have spent every minute with her, watching over her, but he'd taught her to fight. And she had.

She'd fought for her life and for Kristy's. Now Ryder needed to do the same. He needed to fight for his life and for Kristy.

Kristy stood in the vestibule behind where Dean and Ryder sat on the steps. He was going home. She had been worried that might be the case—that once he solved his sister's murder there would be no reason for him to stay at St. Michel's, in Eagle Valley.

Inside the church, just a short while ago, Dean had asked her the same question he had Ryder. He'd wanted to know what her plans were now. She wanted to stay. Despite everything that had happened, she wanted to stay at St. Michel's. She wanted to teach her classes and write and pray…where she felt closest to God, in the little stone church.

There had been some violence inside its walls. Brad's blood stained the stones of the vestibule floor near where she stood. And shots had rung out inside it, boring into seats and the walls. But no stained glass had been broken. No lasting damage had been done.

God had been watching over the church and all of those inside; Brad would be okay. The paramedics had been pretty certain of that before they'd taken him away. And she…

She would be okay now, too.

But she'd rather not be alone. She wanted Ryder to stay. But she could understand that he might need to leave her and all the bad memories of this place behind him. Far behind him…

Would she be just another bad memory for him? Like the memories of his mother's death and Mara's?

Dean glanced back and saw her standing there. "Kristy's staying," he told Ryder. "I think her adjunct professor job will become permanent quite soon. Too bad you're not staying."

"I'm not leaving," Ryder said.

"But you said you're going back to the ranch."

"For a visit," he said. "I haven't taken a vacation in three years. I think I earned some time off."

Dean chuckled. "If that's all it is—"

"It is," Ryder said. "I just want to see my family. Spend some time with them...healing."

Dean reached out and squeezed his shoulder. "You deserve that. I hope you heal now, my friend." He reached up for Kristy's hand and pulled her down next to Ryder. "And I hope you do as well." Then he stood up and walked off into the darkness, no doubt heading toward the administration building. The man was always working.

"You're all right?" Kristy asked. "You didn't get hurt?" She shivered as she remembered all those shots being fired. They'd been so very blessed that nobody had gotten hit...like poor Gretchen had.

Ryder held out his hand with its bloodied and swollen knuckles. "Just this."

She took his hand in hers and held it. "You need an ice pack."

He shook his head. "No. I don't need anything."

"You got justice," she said. "Skip's going away for a long time."

"Because of you," he said.

"It's because of me that he went free for ten years," she said, and her stomach churned yet with how sick she felt over that. She would have to work at forgiving herself, and she doubted Ryder ever would, even after he returned to St. Michel's.

But he didn't pull his hand away from hers. Instead, he entwined their fingers and held on. "A lot of people lied to you," he reminded her. "Skip had many accomplices backing up the story he told you."

"But I should have known the truth," she said. "I knew Mara best. And I let her down."

"Never," he said. "She would have been so proud of you."

Tears stung her eyes.

"You were so strong in that church, so smart to call dispatch like that." He sighed. "He was already trying to weasel out of it again, trying to blame everyone else, but there's the recording now. Even Skip will have to realize he can't buy his way out of trouble this time."

"You always knew," she said. "Your instincts are excellent. Brad said how great a lawman you are. Maybe you should be working for the state police or FBI."

"I enjoy being the campus cowboy cop," he said. "I like it here, and so does Sable."

"You do?" she asked.

He nodded. "I especially like it now that you're here. But I do want to ask you to leave."

She felt a sharp jab to her heart. She'd thought he was forgiving her, that he was even maybe starting to care about her a little. But she should have known it was too much. "Of course," she said. "If it's too hard for you to have me here, I'll leave."

He sucked in a breath then. "You just told Dean you like it here, that you like teaching, but you'd leave if I wanted you to?"

She nodded. "Yes. I don't want to cause you any

more pain. You've been through so much, Ryder. I just want you to be happy."

"Then come to the ranch with me," he said. "Mom would love to see you. And I think you'd be good for my dad. Just like you're good for me."

"Ryder," she murmured, her heart swelling with hope and love. "What are you asking me?"

"To go home with me for a visit, and maybe we can talk Mom and Dad into coming back here to this little church…for our wedding."

"Wedding?"

"I've fallen in love with you, Kristy," he said. "With your goodness, your kindness, your empathy, your positivity. You are amazing."

The tears that had stung her eyes streamed down her face now. She'd wanted his love, so badly, but she hadn't believed it was possible that he would actually fall for her like she'd fallen for him. So hard.

His breath caught, and he cupped her cheek in his palm. "I'm sorry. If you don't feel the same way, I understand. I've done nothing to make you fall for me. I've been so unkind to you. And you never deserved it. You didn't do anything wrong but trust people." He cleared his throat. "So feel free to tell me no. That I've blown it with you."

"That I love you, too," she said. "That's all I want to tell you, Ryder. I love you, too. And you've done so much for me. You saved my life over and over again. But more than that, you saved my very sense of self. For so long I felt lost, like I'd lost who I was…but coming back here, remembering Mara, helped me remember *me*, too. I want to be who I was with Mara—who she was. Strong and fun and fearless."

"You are," he assured her. "You definitely are. You are so strong and so fearless."

"Not sure yet about the fun," she said. "But maybe now that the danger is over, we can find the happiness, just like we found the love. I do love you, Ryder, so very much. And I will go to the ranch with you to visit your folks, and then I want you to meet mine."

Six months later, what Kristy had thought was a fantasy of her overactive imagination came true. Her father walked her down the aisle of that little stone church toward the man standing at the front of it, next to Pastor Howard. Ryder wore a black tuxedo and his black cowboy hat. And the white carnation pinned to his lapel matched the ones in her bouquet and the ones in vases her mom and Becky had placed all over the church.

And as she walked toward her future, Kristy had another fantasy play through her mind: of christening a baby in this church—hers and Ryder's baby—a little girl they would call Mara. And someday, she knew that dream would become a reality, too.

Just like this one…her wedding day.

\* \* \* \* \*

# HARLEQUIN
## PLUS

Try the best multimedia subscription service for romance readers like you!

---

## Read, Watch and Play.

Experience the easiest way to get the romance content you crave.

Start your **FREE TRIAL** at
<u>www.harlequinplus.com/freetrial</u>.